ALEX GILLESPIE

Echoes of Kings Mountain

A Journey of Honor, Hope, and the Fight to Belong

For the Overmountain Men – the farmers, blacksmiths, and sons who left their homes to defend a new nation. May their courage never be forgotten, and their echo never fade from the mountains.

Chapter 1

The first faint light of dawn had not yet broken over the Appalachian ridges when Elias McCrae crept from the cabin. The world outside was a muted canvas of grays and blues, the air crisp enough to bite at exposed skin. He paused at the doorway, one hand resting lightly on the rough pine frame, as if anchoring himself before stepping into the unknown.

Inside, the house breathed with soft, steady rhythms: the low crackle of dying embers in the hearth, his mother's even, quiet breaths, and the slow tick-tock of the hand-carved clock she kept polished. The familiar sounds were a balm and a chain all at once. He swallowed hard, the knot in his throat thickening as he slipped from the threshold into the cold embrace of morning.

The earth beneath his boots was hard with frost, crunching softly with each careful step. Above, the dense canopy of oaks and maples stood still, their bare branches etched against the dim sky. A whippoorwill's mournful call floated through the air—a song of loneliness and warning. Elias paused to listen, feeling the quiet settle deep into his bones.

He fingered the leather straps of his pack, adjusting them until they fit snug against his back. Inside were the essentials: a few hard biscuits wrapped in coarse linen, a half-full powder horn, a small flint and steel, and most precious of all, his brother Samuel's skinning knife. The blade was sheathed in worn leather, its hilt polished smooth by years of use. Elias's fingers brushed the familiar shape, and a flicker of warmth passed through him.

He carried more than gear in that pack. He carried a promise.

Before leaving, he had left a note on the kitchen table, tucked beneath the worn Bible his mother read every night. The ink was still wet, its words scratched with trembling hands:

"I'm sorry, Mama. I have to do this. Please forgive me."

Elias had folded the note twice, then thrice, pressing it flat beneath a heavy stone to keep it from blowing away. He had read and reread those words in the silence of the night, wishing there were a better way to explain the fire inside him, the restless need to join the fight. But no words could carry the weight of his guilt.

He glanced back once more at the cabin. Moonlight spilled through the small windows, casting a pale glow on the worn wooden floorboards. The quilt his mother had sewn—the one embroidered with wildflowers—lay folded neatly on the bed. The scent of pine sap and smoke lingered faintly in the air.

The valley was quiet, but the stillness was deceptive. War was coming, and with it, change that no boy could outrun.

His heart thudded painfully against his ribs as he set off down the narrow path that wound through the thickets and brambles. The trail was faint and overgrown, marked only by broken branches and the occasional rustle of a startled squirrel. The air smelled damp and earthy, mingled with the sharp tang of wild herbs crushed beneath his boots.

As he walked, his thoughts drifted back to the countless evenings he had spent with Samuel. They had been inseparable, brothers not just by blood but by shared dreams. Samuel was the older by three years—stronger, bolder, and already a man in the eyes of their small mountain community.

Elias remembered how Samuel had taught him to hold a rifle, steady and true. How they had practiced in the woods, crafting makeshift targets from bark and tin cans. Samuel's laughter had been easy and infectious, a bright flame that warmed the coldest days. He had been the kind of brother who protected and pushed, who dared Elias to be more than a boy.

But war had stolen him.

News had come one gray afternoon that Samuel's company had been ambushed near Ramseur's Mill. The words had struck like a thunderclap—

men lost, friends fallen, a massacre that left the valley trembling in fear and sorrow. Elias had felt the world tilt beneath his feet. His mother's cries had haunted him, ragged and raw.

Since then, the memory of Samuel's smile haunted him as well—a beacon and a burden. Elias knew that joining the Overmountain Men was the only way to honor that legacy, to turn grief into purpose.

The path grew steeper, winding up toward the ridge where the first pale fingers of sunlight began to bleed through the clouds. Elias paused to catch his breath, the cool wind tugging at his cloak. He looked out over the valley below—the rolling hills quilted with patches of farmland, the winding river like a silver ribbon threading through the earth.

He could almost see the cabins where neighbors and kin still slept, unaware that soon their world would be forever changed.

Ahead, the trail narrowed, skirting a shallow creek where frost glittered like scattered diamonds. The water whispered softly, a gentle lullaby beneath the rustling leaves. Elias knelt and cupped the icy water, drinking deep to still the ache in his throat.

His hands shook as he stood, but he forced himself forward. Each step carried him farther from home and deeper into the promise—and peril—of what lay ahead.

As the sun broke fully over the mountain tops, golden light spilled into the woods. The forest came alive with the chatter of birds and the stir of small creatures. Elias pressed on, feeling the weight of his pack and the hope that it carried.

This was no longer a boy running from fear.

This was a young man stepping into history.

The weight of the pack on his back was nothing compared to the heaviness in Elias's chest as he walked deeper into the forest. The morning light filtered through bare branches, casting long shadows on the leaf-strewn path. But no matter how far he traveled, the ghost of his brother followed close behind.

Samuel's face was the first thing Elias saw whenever his thoughts drifted— sharp jaw, fierce eyes, and that easy smile that once lit every dark corner of their cabin. He remembered the day Samuel left to join the militia, standing tall and proud, his uniform patched but clean, a musket slung over his shoulder. Their mother's tears had fallen quietly then, but Elias had understood. Samuel was going to fight for their land, their freedom, their future.

And Samuel had fought bravely.

Elias's mind replayed the stories whispered through the valley — tales told by men who returned from the frontlines with hollow eyes and heavy hearts. Ramseur's Mill had been a nightmare. An ambush. Friends cut down before they could raise their rifles. Chaos in the smoke and blood. Samuel's name among the fallen. The news had arrived like a thunderclap, shattering the fragile peace of their home.

It was hard to believe Samuel was gone. How could the boy who had taught him to shoot straight be gone? The boy who had laughed so loud, who had promised to bring Elias with him when the time came?

Elias's fingers tightened around the leather strap of the pack, feeling the smooth hilt of Samuel's skinning knife beneath his jacket. It was the last thing his brother had given him before leaving — a symbol of strength, protection, and brotherhood.

The knife was more than a tool; it was a talisman.

Whenever Elias faltered or feared the unknown, he would press his palm against the worn leather sheath and feel an unspoken connection to Samuel. It was as if the blade carried a spark of his brother's courage, a flame to light Elias's darkest moments.

The memory of Samuel was both comfort and torment. It stirred a storm of emotions—pride, grief, anger, and a burning desire to make his brother's sacrifice matter.

Elias thought of his mother, whose quiet strength was bound up in sorrow. She had lost Samuel, but she had not lost hope. Instead, she held onto the fragile belief that Elias's journey might bring justice, might turn the tide of a war that threatened to swallow them whole.

As Elias climbed higher, the wind swept through the pines, carrying with it the scent of earth and cedar. He could almost hear Samuel's voice—a steady, guiding presence that whispered through the rustling leaves.

"Keep your eyes sharp. Trust your heart."

The words echoed in Elias's mind, steady and clear.

He thought back to the evenings when Samuel had sat beside the fire, telling stories of distant battles and dreams of a free land. Those stories had felt like a promise then, a future waiting beyond the mountains.

Now, they were a call to action.

Elias stopped at a rocky outcrop overlooking the valley below, the early morning sun casting a warm glow over the hills. He pulled out a small wooden box he had carved himself, carefully opening it to reveal a worn piece of cloth — a fragment of Samuel's uniform, faded but cherished.

He pressed it to his face, closing his eyes.

"I'll make you proud," he whispered, voice barely audible over the wind.

A single tear traced a path down his cheek, freezing in the cold air. The ache of loss was sharp, but beneath it burned a fierce determination.

Elias slid the cloth back into the box and tucked it safely into his pack. He had no choice but to carry on.

The road ahead was uncertain, full of dangers he could barely imagine. But with Samuel's memory as his guide, Elias felt a flicker of hope.

He would fight. He would survive. And he would honor the brother who had paved the way.

As the sun climbed higher, warming the cold stones beneath his feet, Elias squared his shoulders and pressed forward, the ghost of Samuel walking silently beside him.

The trail beneath Elias's boots wound ever upward, threading through thick groves of oak and chestnut. The earth was damp from last night's rain, and every step stirred the scent of moss and rich soil. His breath came in shallow puffs, mist curling and fading into the morning air as he pressed onward.

The forest was alive in quiet ways: the flutter of a squirrel's tail, the chirp of a bluejay perched high above, the distant rush of a creek tumbling over rocks. But beneath these sounds lay a pulse of something more urgent—a tension that seemed to cling to the very air.

Elias kept his eyes sharp. Each snapped twig or rustled leaf set his heart hammering. Every shadow seemed to hold a secret, every clearing a possible ambush. He knew this was no longer a boy's game.

At a bend in the path, a cold wind whispered through the branches, carrying the faint scent of smoke and distant voices. He paused, chest tight, scanning the horizon. The Overmountain Men were gathering somewhere ahead, their fires marking a gathering place.

But first, the wilderness had tests of its own.

As Elias stepped over a fallen log, his foot caught on a root hidden beneath a blanket of leaves. He stumbled forward, barely catching himself on a nearby tree. His heart skipped a beat, and for a moment, he froze — the crack of a branch underfoot sounding far louder in the silent woods.

He bent down to steady himself, fingers trembling slightly. The pack felt heavier now, the weight of every step pressing down like a stone in his chest. Doubt seeped in, a creeping shadow.

"What am I doing out here?" he whispered, voice breaking the stillness.

But the thought passed quickly, replaced by a hardening resolve. Samuel's knife at his side, the promise to his mother, the memory of his brother's sacrifice — these were the fires stoking his courage.

Elias squared his jaw and pressed forward.

The path narrowed, winding beside a bubbling creek. Frost glittered on rocks, catching the sunlight like scattered jewels. Elias knelt to drink, the cold water biting at his tongue, washing away the taste of fear.

As he rose, a sudden rustling from the bushes startled him. He dropped to one knee, hand slipping toward his knife.

"Easy there," came a voice, low and steady.

From the thicket stepped a young man about Elias's age, with a mop of unruly brown hair and keen gray eyes. He carried a musket slung over his shoulder and wore a patched hunting coat.

"Name's Micah Harper," the stranger said, offering a cautious smile. "Looks like you're headed the same way as me."

Elias relaxed slightly, returning the nod. "Elias McCrae."

Micah stepped closer, eyes flicking to Elias's pack and the knife at his belt.

"You traveling alone?" Micah asked.

"For now."

Micah grinned. "Well, that's no way to go. It's safer in numbers, especially with the Redcoats prowling."

Elias nodded, the tension easing from his shoulders. The promise of companionship was a balm to the loneliness pressing in since he left home.

They walked together along the creek, sharing small talk—their homes, families, reasons for joining the fight. Micah spoke of his sister, who had joined a scout unit, and his uncle, a seasoned ranger under John Sevier.

Elias listened, absorbing the stories, the flicker of hope in Micah's voice.

"Ever been in a fight?" Micah asked, cocking an eyebrow.

Elias shook his head. "No. Just the woods and my rifle."

"Same here," Micah laughed. "Guess we'll both learn fast."

They came to a clearing where the sun spilled through the trees in golden shafts. Micah stopped and pulled out a small bundle of jerky and hardtack, offering some to Elias.

"Take what you can. We'll need our strength."

Gratefully, Elias accepted, breaking off a piece and chewing slowly. The salty taste was a comfort.

They sat for a moment in companionable silence, watching as the forest slowly stirred to life.

Around them, the sounds of the coming day grew louder—a woodpecker's rhythmic tapping, the distant cry of a hawk circling overhead.

Elias thought of home again. Of his mother's gentle hands, the quiet cabin nestled against the mountain's curve, the fields they had tended together. He wondered if she was awake now, worrying, praying.

He wondered if she would forgive him.

Micah's voice broke through the haze.

"Hey, you okay?" he asked, eyes searching Elias's face.

Elias forced a smile. "I will be."

They stood and continued, the path leading upward, steeper now, the air growing thinner and colder.

Elias's legs burned with the effort, but he welcomed it. Each step was a step away from the boy he had been and closer to the man he hoped to become.

The forest opened onto a rocky ridge, where the smell of smoke and woodsmoke grew stronger.

In the distance, he could see flickering campfires and the gathering of men—shapes moving against the early light, the sound of voices rising and falling like a tide.

Elias's heart surged.

This was where the battle would begin.

The scent of smoke grew stronger with every step as Elias and Micah descended the rocky ridge toward the clearing below. The sun had fully risen now, casting long golden fingers across the valley, and the world seemed alive with restless energy.

Ahead, the wide floodplain of Sycamore Shoals stretched out, bordered by thick woods and the winding Watauga River. It was a place familiar to every mountain man and settler in these parts—a natural gathering point where roads converged, where trails from distant homesteads and frontier forts met like the spokes of a great wheel.

But today, the clearing was not quiet. It hummed with the murmur of hundreds of voices—men and boys who, like Elias, had come to answer the call to arms. Rough tents, wagon wagons, and campfires dotted the landscape, the air thick with smoke, sweat, and determination.

Elias's heart hammered fiercely as he stepped onto the soft earth, eyes wide at the throng before him.

Men stood in groups, speaking in low voices or sharpening weapons, their faces weathered and stern. Some laughed quietly, others stared into the distance with grim resolve. There was an electric tension—a mixture of hope and fear that seemed to crackle in the air.

Micah clapped Elias on the shoulder. "Welcome to Sycamore Shoals," he said with a grin. "This is where legends are born."

Elias swallowed hard, suddenly aware of how small and uncertain he felt amid this surge of men hardened by the wilderness and war.

He followed Micah toward a cluster of familiar faces—veterans and local leaders who had been organizing the muster. Among them was John Sevier, a tall, broad-shouldered man with steely eyes and a voice that commanded respect. His presence was magnetic, the kind that made men listen and follow.

Beside Sevier stood Isaac Shelby, quieter but no less formidable, his expression calm and calculating.

Micah nodded toward the two leaders. "These are the men who'll lead us into battle."

Elias studied them, trying to steady his racing pulse. He imagined the stories he had heard—the daring raids, the brutal skirmishes, the relentless march through mountains and rivers.

The men around him spoke of Patriot cause, of the tyranny of the Crown, and of the freedom they hoped to secure for their families and homes. Elias could feel the weight of their convictions pressing on his young shoulders.

As they moved deeper into the camp, Elias caught sight of faces filled with determination and sorrow. There were seasoned hunters with rifles slung low, farmers clutching homemade muskets, and boys barely older than Elias himself, clutching worn knives and buckskin pouches.

Some had lost fathers, brothers, or sons in this fight. Others had seen their homes burned or their crops destroyed by the enemy.

A hush fell over the crowd as John Sevier raised his voice, calling the men together for a council.

Elias edged closer, pushing through the throng, his breath caught in his throat.

Sevier's voice was steady and commanding as he spoke of the battle ahead, of the need for courage and unity. He outlined the plan—to cross the rugged mountains, to strike the Loyalist forces gathered at King's Mountain, and to break the enemy's hold on the frontier.

The men listened intently, nodding in agreement or murmuring assent. Some clenched their fists, others exchanged determined glances.

Elias's heart pounded louder than ever. He was no longer just a boy with a pack and a knife. He was part of something larger—a movement, a fight for freedom and justice.

Micah leaned in, whispering, "This is it, Elias. The moment we've been waiting for."

Elias nodded, swallowing the lump in his throat.

Around the campfires, conversations buzzed with plans and promises. Men traded stories of past battles and speculated on what lay ahead. Elias found himself drawn into a small group of young men who shared his age, their eyes bright with a mix of fear and excitement.

One introduced himself as Jacob, a sharpshooter from Virginia. Another was Thomas, a blacksmith's son like Elias, whose hands were already calloused from labor and training.

They spoke of families left behind, of dreams for a free future, and of the price they knew they might pay.

Elias felt the knot of loneliness begin to loosen, replaced by a fierce sense of belonging.

Later, as the sun dipped toward the horizon, Elias found a quiet spot near the riverbank. He pulled out the wooden box containing Samuel's uniform fragment and held it close.

The faces of the men in camp flickered like shadows in the firelight, each carrying their own hopes and fears.

Elias whispered a silent vow: *I will not fail you, Samuel. I will carry your fight.*

The camp was alive with the sounds of preparation—the steady beat of hammer on anvil, the rustle of fabric as men patched their clothes, the murmur of prayers whispered into the night.

Above, the stars began to pierce the darkening sky, a cold wind sweeping down from the mountains.

Elias tucked the box away and looked up, feeling the vastness of the world beyond the firelight.

This was the beginning. The first step on a path that would test every ounce of courage he had.

And as the night deepened, he knew that when the time came, he would stand beside these men, with the memory of Samuel burning bright in his heart.

The night before the march was restless. The camp at Sycamore Shoals was alive with quiet preparation—the soft murmur of voices, the scraping of feet on dirt, the occasional crackle of firewood. Shadows danced among tents and wagons as men sharpened blades, cleaned muskets, and said hurried prayers.

Elias lay on a bed of pine boughs beneath the stars, the wooden box with Samuel's cloth clutched tightly in his hands. His thoughts raced between hope and fear, the weight of what was to come settling heavily on his young shoulders.

Sleep was a stranger, slipping away each time the wind stirred the leaves or a distant shout echoed through the camp.

Before dawn, a sudden shout broke the uneasy calm.

"Enemy sighted!"

Men scrambled to their feet, grabbing weapons and rushing toward the camp's edge. Elias's heart leapt into his throat as the first flashes of musket fire cracked through the pre-dawn gloom.

Chaos erupted.

Orders rang out—sharp and urgent.

"Form ranks! Hold the line!"

Elias stumbled to his feet, hands shaking as he gripped his rifle. His breath came fast, lungs burning in the cold air. Around him, men surged forward, faces grim and eyes wide with adrenaline.

The first clash was violent and swift.

From the tree line emerged a group of Loyalist scouts, their red coats gleaming faintly in the dim light. They fired their muskets, then charged with bayonets drawn.

Elias fired his rifle, the recoil jolting his shoulder. The sound was deafening, ringing in his ears like thunder. Smoke curled from the barrel, mixing with the sharp smell of gunpowder.

He saw a man fall near him, clutching his side, blood darkening his shirt. The sight twisted something inside Elias—a knot of terror and determination.

This was no longer a story told around campfires. This was real.

The clash of steel and roar of musket fire filled the clearing as the Overmountain Men pushed back the attackers. Men shouted, bullets whistled past, and the ground seemed to tremble beneath their feet.

Elias's rifle cracked again and again, each shot shaking his nerves and resolve. His hands moved on their own, guided by training and fear.

Nearby, Micah fought fiercely, his musket swinging to strike a Loyalist before firing another shot. "Stay with me, Elias!" he shouted.

Elias swallowed his panic and nodded, forcing his eyes to focus beyond the chaos. The enemy was pressing hard, and the men's lines wavered.

Suddenly, a Loyalist broke through the front, charging toward Elias with a bayonet raised. Time slowed.

Elias dropped to one knee, raising his rifle like a club. The man lunged.

The crack of wood meeting flesh echoed sharply as Elias's rifle barrel smashed into the attacker's face. The man staggered, blood pouring from a split brow, and collapsed.

Elias's breath came in ragged gasps. His heart thundered wildly.

"Good shot!" Micah called, clapping him on the shoulder. "You did good."

But Elias barely heard him. The reality of taking a life—or nearly doing so—sent a cold shiver through his veins.

He knelt there for a moment, chest heaving, eyes wide as the smoke cleared.

The battle ebbed and flowed. The Loyalists regrouped and charged again, but the Overmountain Men held firm, their determination unbreakable.

Elias found himself moving with a strange clarity amidst the madness. His fears receded, replaced by a fierce focus. Every muscle ached, every nerve screamed—but he fought on.

Around him, men cheered as the attackers finally broke and fled into the woods.

The clearing fell silent except for ragged breaths and the soft moans of the wounded.

Elias sank to the ground, knees trembling. Blood stained his hands—some his own, some another's.

Micah sat beside him, wiping sweat and grime from his face. "You alright?"

Elias nodded slowly, still trying to steady his racing heart.

"I think so," he said quietly.

The first blood had been spilled. The cost of freedom had revealed itself in brutal clarity.

Elias glanced toward the rising sun, its light cutting through the smoke and shadows.

He thought of Samuel again, of the path his brother had walked—and the path Elias had now chosen.

The battle was only beginning.

Chapter 2

An early glow of morning filtered weakly through the thick canopy of Sycamore Shoals, casting pale shadows over the restless camp. The night's chill still lingered in the air, wrapping the forest in a fragile silence that belied the storm brewing beneath.

Elias stirred beneath his worn blanket, muscles aching from the day's march and the violent clash that had shattered their peace. The rough pine boughs beneath him offered little comfort, but sleep had been fleeting—haunted by flashes of musket fire, cries of the wounded, and the cold stare of the Loyalist he had struck down.

His fingers trembled as they brushed against the wooden box tucked beside him. Inside lay the small scrap of Samuel's uniform, worn and frayed but heavy with meaning. Elias's heart ached with longing and guilt. *This fight is for you,* he whispered silently, eyes closing as memories of his brother's voice filled the quiet.

Around the camp, men stirred to life. Soft voices whispered prayers and shared whispered comforts. The campfires, now reduced to glowing embers, flared anew as logs were added, casting flickering light over weary faces.

Near Elias, a man named Caleb sat hunched over his rifle. His gray-streaked beard was tangled and unkempt, but his eyes held a steady calm. Elias had learned Caleb was a veteran of earlier frontier battles, a man who had seen the land's worst and lived to tell its tale.

Caleb glanced up and caught Elias's gaze. "First night's never easy," he said quietly. "You'll carry those sights with you longer than you expect."

Elias nodded, swallowing hard. "I didn't think... it would be like that."

Caleb's lips tightened. "None of us do, boy. But you survived. That's the start."

A gentle breeze stirred the camp, carrying the scent of damp earth, pine needles, and the faint, metallic tang of blood. The smell lingered in Elias's nostrils like a stubborn ghost.

Micah emerged from his tent, rubbing his eyes but wearing a determined expression. "Rise and shine, Elias. Today we start the march in earnest. King's Mountain won't wait."

The words settled heavily on Elias's chest. The first battle was only a taste of what was to come.

As men gathered for breakfast, a makeshift meal of hardtack and salted pork, Elias spotted two new faces weaving through the crowd.

One was a scout named Daniel, slender and quick, with sharp eyes that missed little. His clothes were worn but practical, and he carried a small bundle of maps and notes tied with leather straps.

Beside him walked Martha, a healer from the nearby settlement. Her hands were steady and sure, and her presence brought a sense of calm. Elias had heard whispers that she was known for tending wounds that others wouldn't dare touch, and her skill was already respected among the men.

Daniel stopped at the leaders' tent, unrolling his maps with a practiced hand. John Sevier leaned in, studying the terrain lines and enemy positions.

Martha moved quietly among the wounded, offering water and bandages, her voice soft but firm.

Elias felt a growing respect for both—each vital in ways beyond the musket's fire.

The camp buzzed with cautious energy as preparations began. Horses were saddled, weapons cleaned, and orders repeated. The air was thick with the mix of anticipation and dread that only soldiers know before a long march into uncertain battle.

Elias found a quiet moment near the river, watching the water rush past stones worn smooth by time. The flow was steady and unyielding, like the tide of events drawing him forward.

Memories of home tugged at him. The warmth of his mother's smile, the steady hammer of his father's forge, the laughter of younger siblings playing among the trees. Those images were distant now, like ghosts slipping through his fingers.

But Samuel's face remained sharp and clear—the brother he had lost but refused to forget.

Elias touched the box again, a silent promise etched into his soul.

"Ready for this?" Micah's voice startled him.

Elias turned to see his friend watching with a hard, honest look.

"I think I have to be," Elias replied. "No matter what."

Micah nodded, clapping him on the shoulder. "Good. Because once we leave this clearing, it's a long road. And we'll need every bit of strength."

As the sun climbed higher, the men gathered in tighter formation. Leaders addressed the group, their voices steady despite the weight of responsibility.

Sevier's gaze swept the crowd. "We march not just for ourselves, but for every family that calls these mountains home. For the freedom to live without fear of tyranny. Today, we take one more step toward that dream."

A cheer rose from the men, voices rough but fierce with conviction.

Elias felt a swell of pride mixed with a cold knot of fear.

The march would test them all—not just their bodies, but their spirits.

And in the quiet moments before the first step, Elias knew he would carry Samuel's memory with him—fuel for the fight, a beacon in the darkest hours.

The sun blazed overhead as the column began to move, the rhythm of footsteps echoing through the forest.

The battle for their future had only just begun.

The column moved steadily through the dense forest, the muffled crunch of boots on leaf-strewn earth blending with the occasional snap of a twig. The morning sun filtered through towering oaks and pines, dappling the narrow trail ahead with shifting patches of gold and shadow.

Elias kept pace beside Micah, his breath coming hard but steady. Every muscle ached from the previous day's skirmish and the long hours of preparation, but the resolve in the men's eyes pushed him onward.

Around them, the march stretched in both directions—a river of determined faces framed by weathered rifles, leather satchels, and dust-streaked clothing. Some hummed old folk tunes, others murmured prayers or exchanged quiet words.

The wilderness pressed close on every side, its tangled underbrush a reminder of the dangers lurking beyond just enemy soldiers. Rattlesnakes, bears, and the unforgiving land itself were constant threats.

Elias felt the weight of his rifle digging into his shoulder with every step, but it was the heaviness in his chest that he struggled with most.

Memories flooded him—his mother's gentle hands teaching him to read, the sharp clang of his father's hammer shaping iron, and most of all, Samuel's laughter echoing through the family's cabin.

He swallowed the lump forming in his throat and focused on the path.

Micah glanced over, sensing Elias's silence. "You thinking about home?"

Elias nodded. "Every step. I miss it more than I thought I would."

Micah smiled faintly. "Aye. But this—this fight's for all that. For home, for family, for a future free of fear."

The trail wound upward, steepening as the men climbed rocky slopes and crossed rushing creeks. Sweat soaked Elias's shirt, stinging his eyes, but the thought of turning back never crossed his mind.

Midway through the morning, the column paused beside a broad clearing where the sun warmed the earth. Men dropped packs and shared scraps of food, some tending blisters and sore feet.

Elias sank onto a moss-covered log, grateful for the brief respite.

Nearby, a man named Thomas, broad-shouldered and grizzled, shared a tale of his time fighting in Virginia. His voice was gruff but lively, painting vivid pictures of smoky battlefields and narrow escapes.

Elias listened, captivated, as Thomas spoke of loyalty, sacrifice, and the cost of freedom.

"War's a cruel master," Thomas said, wiping sweat from his brow. "But sometimes, it's the only way to make a mark, to stand for something bigger than yourself."

Elias nodded slowly, absorbing the weight of those words.

As the men rested, Elias struck up conversation with Daniel, the scout introduced the day before. Daniel's sharp eyes and quiet confidence had already earned him respect.

"The woods are alive with movement," Daniel said, pointing to a nearby thicket. "Enemy scouts have been spotted ahead. They know we're coming."

Elias felt a shiver run through him.

"How do we stop them?" he asked.

Daniel shrugged. "We move fast, stay alert. We can't afford to give them a chance."

The conversation drifted toward tactics and survival, and Elias felt himself growing sharper, more aware.

Yet beneath the surface, tension simmered. Whispers of disagreement about leadership had begun to circulate, and small groups formed with murmured debates.

Some men questioned Sevier's boldness; others worried about the risks of marching so close to Loyalist territory. Arguments about strategy and the spoils of victory flickered like embers in the camp.

Elias caught a heated exchange between two men near the fire that evening—one insisting on caution, the other urging swift attack.

The discord unsettled him, a reminder that even in unity, the cause was not without its fractures.

That night, as Elias settled beneath the stars once more, he found himself wrestling with doubts.

Could they truly win this fight? Were their differences too great? And most terrifying of all—was he strong enough to carry the burdens ahead?

He pulled the wooden box close, the worn fabric inside a talisman against despair.

Tomorrow would bring more trials. But for now, Elias closed his eyes and clung to hope.

The sun was just breaking over the horizon when the scouts returned, their horses kicking up dust on the worn trail leading back to camp. Elias spotted Daniel among them, his face drawn tight with urgency. The other riders rode in silence, their eyes scanning the forest like hawks.

A ripple of unease passed through the camp as the men gathered near the command tent, the usual morning chatter replaced by whispered questions and anxious glances. John Sevier and the other leaders stood waiting, faces etched with tension.

Daniel dismounted, his boots hitting the ground with a heavy thud. He wasted no time, unrolling his maps and pointing out positions and movements with a trembling finger.

"Loyalist forces have been spotted just beyond Pine Ridge," Daniel reported, his voice low but clear. "They've doubled their patrols and are setting traps along the northern pass."

Sevier's jaw clenched. "Are they aware of our presence?"

"Not fully," Daniel answered. "But they're closing in fast. If we don't move carefully, we risk walking into an ambush."

The leaders exchanged grave looks. For the men already weary from their march, this news was a sharp reminder of the danger pressing on all sides.

Elias lingered near the edge of the gathering, listening intently. The urgency in Daniel's voice stirred a mix of fear and adrenaline in him—a feeling both familiar and foreign.

After the meeting broke up, Elias found himself drawn to a small group huddled near the fire. Among them was Rebecca, a quiet but sharp-eyed woman who had joined the fight after her family's farm was seized. She leaned in, her voice low and urgent.

"There's more at stake than just this fight," she whispered. "Some say there are spies in our midst, even among those we call friends."

Elias's heart quickened. "Spies? Here?"

Rebecca nodded grimly. "Trust is fragile. We have to be careful who we confide in. The enemy is clever, and they use every trick to tear us apart."

Elias frowned. "Do you think someone here would betray us?"

Rebecca's eyes darted around, then she lowered her voice further. "I don't know for sure. But I've heard things—strange movements at night, whispers that don't match the men's usual talk. We can't afford to be blind."

A pang of fear tightened in Elias's chest. If the enemy had infiltrated their camp, every step could be a trap, every word a risk.

Later, Elias sought out Caleb, hoping the veteran's experience might ease his troubled mind.

"Spies, secrets... war's full of shadows," Caleb said, his voice gravelly but steady as they sat near the dying embers of a fire. "But it's trust and loyalty that keep men alive. You watch your back, but you don't lose faith in your brothers."

Elias swallowed hard. "How do you know who to trust?"

Caleb's eyes narrowed. "Sometimes you don't. You listen, you watch, you feel. There's no foolproof way. But you hold onto what you believe is right, and you keep moving forward."

Elias exhaled slowly, the veteran's words both a comfort and a challenge.

As the day wore on, Elias felt the weight of uncertainty press harder. The forest around them seemed to whisper warnings through the rustling leaves and shifting light. Each step forward was met with both hope and hesitation.

During a brief rest, Elias's thoughts drifted back to Samuel once more. He recalled the quiet nights beside the forge, the stories Samuel had told of frontier life and the fight for justice. Those memories, vivid and warm, were both comforting and tormenting.

A pang of doubt gnawed at him. Was he truly ready for this? Could he face the challenges that lay ahead, not just from enemies, but from within?

The leaders called a meeting beneath a sprawling oak, its branches wide and sheltering. Sevier spoke with a calm authority, laying out plans for the coming days.

"We move with caution but resolve," he said. "Our strength is in our unity. We watch for traps, we protect each other. And we strike when the moment is right."

Elias studied the faces around him—the hard-set eyes, the scars of past battles, the flickers of hope. In that moment, he understood that this fight was not just about muskets or territory. It was a test of character, of courage in the face of fear.

That night, as the camp settled once more, Elias lay beneath the stars, the wooden box at his side. His thoughts tumbled between hope and worry, loyalty and suspicion.

He stared at the sky, tracing constellations his father had taught him long ago. *Keep your eyes open,* his father's voice echoed in his mind. *Trust your heart, but watch for shadows.*

Beneath it all burned a fierce determination. No matter the secrets or shadows, he would carry on. For Samuel. For home. For freedom.

The forest grew darker as the afternoon sun slipped behind thickening clouds. A restless murmur ran through the camp like a low thunder, heavy with uncertainty. The men gathered around fires and whispered in tight clusters, voices hushed but tense.

Elias felt the undercurrent of unease settle into his bones. Every crackle of leaves, every distant birdcall seemed to hint at unseen dangers lurking just beyond sight.

The camp was alive with a restless energy, nerves stretched taut. The news of spies and the approaching Loyalist patrols had unsettled even the bravest among them. Arguments flared quietly here and there, and the once unshakeable camaraderie now showed small cracks.

John Sevier paced near the command tent, his jaw tight, eyes scanning the crowd as if he could see the threat before it materialized. His usual calm and confidence had been replaced by a fierce determination, but even he could not mask the growing tension.

Elias caught sight of Micah speaking quietly with Caleb, their faces serious. When their eyes met, Elias nodded, sensing the weight they both carried.

Later, the leaders convened beneath the oak tree where they had gathered the day before. The men formed a rough circle, the air thick with anticipation.

Sevier cleared his throat, silencing the murmurs.

"We've received more reports," he began, voice steady despite the urgency beneath it. "Loyalist patrols are increasing in size and boldness. Their scouts are probing our positions, testing our defenses. It's clear they aim to cut us off before we can reach the mountain passes."

A ripple of unease swept through the group.

"We face two choices," Sevier continued. "We can press on cautiously, risking an ambush. Or we can move quickly, striking hard before they can fully organize."

His gaze swept the circle.

"Some of you have suggested an immediate attack. Others urge patience. I want to hear from you."

Hands rose, voices rose with them—some calling for bold action, others warning against recklessness.

Elias watched as the debate grew heated. The men argued not just over tactics, but over what kind of future they wanted to build. Some feared the fight might cost them everything; others believed without risk, there was no hope.

Micah's voice cut through the rising clamor. "We must remember why we march. Our homes, our families, our very freedom depend on what we do next. We can't afford to let fear decide for us."

The group fell silent at his words.

Sevier nodded approvingly. "Well said, Micah. We will move at dawn. We strike before the Loyalists can mount a full defense."

The decision was made. The men dispersed, preparing quietly for the night ahead.

Elias felt a surge of adrenaline and fear. The coming hours would test all they had learned—and all they were willing to risk.

That evening, as campfires flickered and shadows danced, Elias found himself wandering away from the bustle to a quiet clearing. The moon cast pale light through the trees, painting silver patterns on the ground.

He took out the wooden box, tracing its worn edges with trembling fingers. Inside, the keepsakes from Samuel—a folded letter, a carved wooden token, a small knife—reminded him of the brother he had lost and the promise he had made.

The distant sounds of men singing faintly carried on the breeze, voices weaving stories of home, loss, and hope.

Elias's thoughts were interrupted by the soft footsteps of Rebecca. She settled beside him, her eyes reflecting the pale moonlight.

"You're carrying a heavy burden," she said gently.

He nodded. "Every step feels heavier than the last. I wonder if I'm strong enough."

Rebecca smiled faintly. "Strength isn't just muscle or firepower. It's standing up when you're afraid. It's holding onto hope even when shadows close in."

They sat together in silence, the weight of the night settling over them.

After a moment, Rebecca spoke again. "I've heard whispers about a man—one of our own—who might be working for the Loyalists. We don't know who, but it's tearing us apart."

Elias's heart raced. "How can we fight if the enemy is inside?"

Rebecca shrugged. "We watch. We listen. We trust our instincts. And we stay united."

Their conversation was interrupted by a sudden shout from the camp.

"Patrol's sighted!" someone called.

The camp erupted into motion. Men grabbed weapons, hurried to their positions, and called out orders.

Elias's heart pounded as he sprinted back toward the command tent. Flames from torches pierced the night, illuminating faces etched with determination and fear.

Sevier's voice rang out. "Stay calm! Form ranks! Protect the camp!"

From the shadows, shapes moved—figures darting between trees, elusive and dangerous.

Elias gripped his rifle tightly, scanning the darkness.

A sharp whistle cut through the air, followed by a flurry of musket fire.

The battle had begun.

Amidst the chaos, Elias found himself fighting not just for survival, but for every promise he'd made—to his brother, to his friends, to the land they all loved.

The gathering storm had broken. And there was no turning back.

The forest was eerily silent after the musket fire faded, leaving only the crackling of small fires and the distant calls of night birds. The men stood scattered among the trees, breaths heavy, bodies tense. The flickering torchlight cast long shadows on faces grim with exhaustion and fear.

Elias knelt beside a wounded comrade, pressing a cloth to a bleeding arm.

The man's teeth clenched in pain, but his eyes met Elias's with steady gratitude. Around them, others tended to injuries or kept watch, alert for any further attack.

The skirmish had been brief but fierce—a stark reminder that danger lurked even when the night seemed calm. The Loyalist patrol had struck swiftly, testing their defenses, then vanished like ghosts into the woods.

Sevier moved among the men, offering quiet words of encouragement, his presence a steady anchor in the chaos. His broad shoulders bore the weight of command, yet Elias noticed the deep lines of fatigue carved into his face.

Elias's thoughts whirled. The attack was a brutal wake-up call. They were not just marching toward a goal—they were entering a war, one with no easy victories or guarantees.

As dawn broke, pale light filtered through the trees, revealing the toll of the fight. Wounded men lay on blankets, some moaning softly, others staring blankly into the sky. The camp was somber, shadows deeper than before.

Elias found a moment alone by the river that curved near their camp. The cool water rippled gently, reflecting the soft pinks and blues of the early morning sky. He cupped his hands, splashing water on his face, trying to wash away the grime—and the fear—that clung to him.

The wooden box from Samuel sat by his side, its weight heavier now. Elias thought about his brother's quiet strength, his unwavering belief in justice and freedom. He wondered what Samuel would say if he could see this—this messy, painful fight for something bigger than themselves.

"You carry a heavy load, Elias."

Elias turned to see Caleb approaching, his face lined with exhaustion but eyes steady.

"I'm not sure I'm ready for this," Elias admitted. "I thought I was... but now—"

Caleb rested a firm hand on his shoulder. "No one is ever truly ready. But you're here, and you're fighting. That counts for more than you think."

They stood in silence, the river's steady flow a quiet reminder of time passing, of life moving forward even in the darkest moments.

Back in camp, the leaders gathered again, planning their next move. The attack had changed everything. They knew the Loyalists would not stop until this land was theirs.

Sevier's voice was resolute. "We push on. We learn from this. Every scar is a lesson. And we will need every one of you—every ounce of courage and strength."

Elias listened, feeling the weight of those words settle deep inside him. The march was no longer just a journey; it was a battle for survival, for identity, for the very soul of their homeland.

That afternoon, the camp was a flurry of activity. Men helped carry the wounded to safer spots, while others gathered wood and water, trying to restore some semblance of order and comfort. The air smelled of smoke, blood, and earth — raw reminders of the night's violence.

Elias found himself drawn to the small infirmary tent where a young soldier lay with a shattered arm. The boy's face was pale, his eyes wide with shock.

"It'll heal," Elias said softly, gripping the boy's shoulder. "We'll make sure of it."

The boy nodded, biting his lip against the pain. Elias knew the road ahead would be long—not just for the body, but for the spirit.

Nearby, Rebecca helped tend to an older man whose face was streaked with dirt and sweat. She caught Elias's eye and gave a small, tired smile. "We're stronger than we know," she said quietly.

Later, Elias gathered with Caleb and Micah near the fire. The three men shared a meal in silence, the weight of the night's events pressing down like a heavy cloak.

Caleb broke the silence. "This fight is bigger than any one of us. It's about what kind of world we want to live in. Freedom isn't given—it's taken."

Micah nodded. "We carry the hopes of our families, our homes, and all who've been wronged. Every step forward is for them."

Elias felt a spark of resolve kindle inside him. The fear that had gripped him earlier was replaced by a fierce determination. He would not let the darkness consume them.

That night, as the camp settled, Elias lay beneath the stars once more. The wooden box was at his side, a tangible link to Samuel and the past they both carried.

He traced the carvings on the token, feeling the rough edges beneath his fingertips.

Whispers of doubt still lingered, but beneath them was something stronger—a promise forged in fire and blood.

No matter what lay ahead, Elias knew he would fight. For Samuel. For home. For freedom.

Chapter 3

Over the ridge, the sun emerged, it's long golden beams gliding across frost-bitten grass and sleeping men. The morning was silent but for the slow rustle of canvas and the clink of tin cups as the Overmountain Men stirred from a hard-won sleep. Elias sat on a moss-covered rock near the edge of camp, chewing a strip of dried venison and staring out into the shifting mists. He hadn't slept much. The echo of the skirmish still rang in his mind—musket blasts, cries in the dark, the awful stillness that followed.

They had survived, but the price lingered in the air like gunpowder.

A bugle call, sharp and clear, broke the morning calm. It wasn't meant to rouse the enemy—it was for the living. A signal to rise and move, to press forward, wounded and whole alike. Elias stood, stretched the stiffness from his limbs, and adjusted the leather strap across his shoulder. His satchel dug into his side, but he welcomed the ache. It meant he was still here.

Caleb passed him with a nod, already saddled and walking his mare beside him. "Another day, another blister."

Elias smiled faintly. "I think I'm growing new feet just to keep up with the old ones."

The two fell into step as the men began forming up, their numbers ragged but resolute. Rebecca moved through the crowd, checking bandages and offering bits of food and warmth where she could. She looked tired, her braid fraying and dark circles beneath her eyes, but she never stopped moving. When she caught Elias looking, she gave a quiet nod, the kind that said *We're still here. Keep going.*

The trail ahead twisted through the foothills like a scar. Fallen leaves turned the path slick underfoot, and the steep climbs sapped the strength from even the most seasoned frontiersmen. Elias stumbled more than once, but he never let himself fall behind. Each step was a word in a promise—a promise he'd made silently that he'd see this through, no matter the cost.

Around midday, the march halted briefly at a ridge overlooking a narrow valley. Trees lined the edge, their branches nearly bare, trembling in the wind like skeletal fingers. Below, a slow-moving creek shimmered in the sun.

Sevier and Shelby stood ahead, conferring over maps and terrain. The two commanders had grown graver by the day. Scouts had returned with troubling reports—Loyalist activity was increasing, and British regulars weren't far behind. If Ferguson's army crossed the mountains ahead of them, it could trap the Patriot militia between the ridgelines.

"We move fast," Sevier said loud enough for the line officers to hear. "And we move quiet. We don't want to be caught where the rocks narrow and there's no turning back."

The men refilled their canteens, checked their gear, and started forward again. The trail narrowed as they descended, the earth soft from recent rains. Roots snaked across the path, and thorns reached out to tear at their sleeves. At one point, Elias slipped on a patch of wet clay and landed hard on his hands. Caleb helped him up without a word.

His palms were streaked with blood and dirt, but he clenched them into fists and kept walking.

By late afternoon, the hills grew steeper. Every upward slope burned his calves, and every breath came with the chill bite of mountain air. The old men said this was the hard part—that after this came the worst of it. Elias didn't ask what that meant. He didn't want to know.

Behind them, somewhere in the folds of the hills, rode death. Ferguson's men weren't ghosts. They were flesh and blood, steel and fire. And they were hunting.

As the sky faded to orange and then bruised purple, the line of men reached a small plateau dotted with deadfall and scrub pine. There was enough flat ground for fires and tents, and enough tree cover to keep the wind at bay.

Elias collapsed onto a log, heart pounding. He peeled off his boots and winced at the blisters blooming across his feet. Caleb tossed him a ragged cloth and a salve that smelled of pine and vinegar.

"Use this," he said. "It won't make 'em pretty, but it'll keep you walking."

"Thanks." Elias took it gratefully. "How do you keep going?"

Caleb shrugged. "Because the only other choice is stopping. And stopping means being buried in these hills before the leaves finish falling."

Elias stared into the forest beyond the firelight. Every crack of a branch felt like a threat, every gust of wind a whisper from the Loyalist lines. He wondered how many boys like him sat around fires tonight on the other side—cold, hungry, afraid. Did they think about home? Did they have brothers they'd buried or sisters waiting by the door?

The thought chilled him more than the mountain wind.

He reached into his satchel and pulled out the wooden box. His fingers brushed over the carvings—Samuel's mark. The lid creaked as he opened it, revealing the contents he knew by heart: the token carved from ash, the folded letter, the tiny knife with the worn hilt. Each item a tether to the world he'd left behind.

He didn't read the letter. Not yet. He wasn't ready. But he needed to know it was there.

The fire cracked, sparks rising like stars into the cold night. Around him, the Overmountain Men whispered, sharpened blades, counted powder, and prayed in low voices. Some joked to break the tension. Others stared silently into the flames.

They were not the same men who had set out from Watauga. The march had begun with pride and purpose. Now, there was a hard edge to it—a grim understanding that many of them would not return.

Elias leaned back against his pack and watched the stars come out, one by one. The war was drawing them onward like a storm cloud over the next ridge. But tonight, for a moment, he allowed himself to feel the ground beneath him, the ache in his legs, the thrum of blood in his ears.

He was alive.

And tomorrow, they would march again.

Morning broke not with birdsong or warmth, but with brittle wind and the crunch of frost underfoot. Elias woke to find his blanket stiff with ice, his breath hanging in pale clouds above his head. Around him, the camp stirred slowly, stiff-backed and bleary-eyed. Joints popped as men rolled up bedrolls, and quiet curses followed the snapping of frozen bootstraps. No one laughed this morning. The cold had stripped them down to bone and will.

Elias stood by the fire pit with Caleb, holding his tin cup close to the coals. The brew inside was little more than warm water tinged with bark and dandelion root, but it eased the ache in his chest and thawed his fingers. Rebecca handed out the last of the dried berries and reminded the men to chew them slowly. "Too fast and you'll spend half the day doubled over."

She flashed Elias a tired smile, but he could see the weight in her eyes. The march was wearing on everyone. Still, no one turned back.

As they set out again, Elias noted the subtle shift in their ranks. Men who once laughed together now marched in silence. Officers who shared flasks days ago now eyed one another with stiff, guarded expressions. Word of disagreements between the leaders had begun to ripple through the company, whispered during halts or passed quietly around the campfires.

It wasn't long before the tension came to a head.

The trail that morning cut through a narrow gap between two steep ridgelines. Dense thickets pressed in from both sides, turning the column into a single file line. The horses struggled in the mud, and the footmen were forced to weave around slick roots and sunken stones. When they finally emerged into a wider clearing by midday, the grumbling began in earnest.

"Fool's path," muttered one man ahead of Elias. "Could've saved a mile turning east by the creek bed."

Another answered, "We'd've been in sight of the Loyalists, and you know it."

"Only if they're still behind us," the first snapped. "You trust Sevier's scouts that much?"

That name—Sevier—turned more than a few heads.

Up near the front of the line, a knot of men had stopped altogether, crowding around a flat stone where Shelby and Sevier were hunched over a map. Elias edged forward, pulled by curiosity. He wasn't the only one. Others slowed their pace to listen in, and soon a circle formed, thinly veiled as rest but thick with scrutiny.

"We need to cross here before nightfall," Sevier was saying, tapping the parchment with a calloused finger. "If we wait, the pass could flood."

Shelby frowned. "And leave the supply train behind? Half our men are still an hour back, struggling through the muck."

"We don't have time to wait for every wagon," Sevier snapped. "You saw the scout reports. Ferguson's less than two days out."

"And what would you have us do?" Shelby asked coldly. "Leave the wounded to fend for themselves?"

Sevier's eyes narrowed. "I'd have us reach King's Mountain before we're fighting uphill with our backs to a ravine."

"Gentlemen," came the cool voice of Colonel Campbell, stepping between them. His white hair glinted in the sunlight. "We are one force with one purpose. The enemy is not here among us."

The tension crackled like dry leaves. Shelby said nothing for a long moment, then nodded stiffly and turned back toward the trail. Sevier rolled the map up with a snap and stalked off in the opposite direction.

The crowd began to move again, but the damage had been done. Murmurs followed them down the slope, whispers of discord that Elias could feel in his chest like a drumbeat. It frightened him more than the enemy. If they couldn't hold together now, what chance did they have when the bullets flew?

That afternoon, the trail forked near an abandoned hunting cabin. The structure was little more than a collapsed roof and a moss-covered chimney, but it provided a natural landmark. The company split briefly to search the area and regroup. Elias was assigned to a scouting party led by a grizzled man named Buck Withers, a former trapper with a voice like gravel and a permanent scowl etched into his face.

Withers didn't speak much, but he moved like he knew every root and shadow. Elias tried to keep up, heart pounding in his throat as they hiked a steep slope to get a better view of the valley below. From the crest, the world stretched out in endless folds—pine and shadow, creek beds winding like silver veins. No sign of Ferguson. Not yet.

Back at the cabin ruins, Elias sat beside Caleb, who was rubbing oil into his musket's lockplate. "You saw them arguing," Elias said. "Sevier and Shelby."

Caleb nodded. "Aye. They're both proud men, and this march is testing every inch of their patience."

"But they're on the same side."

Caleb looked at him. "That don't always make it easier. Pride's a sharp thing. Easier to point it at your brother than your enemy."

Elias was quiet a moment. "You think they'll split?"

Caleb blew on the musket's trigger. "I think they won't. Because they know what happens if they do."

The younger men nearby were restless—drumming fingers on canteens, muttering into the cold wind. Some questioned the path. Others doubted the cause. Elias heard one say he'd had enough and would head home at first light. He didn't know if the man meant it, but he saw how the words unsettled the others. Uncertainty spreads like smoke—quick, choking, invisible until it's everywhere.

Before nightfall, Colonel Campbell gathered them all. The commanders stood on a rise, backlit by the setting sun.

"We do not all come from the same colony," Campbell began, voice strong. "We are Virginians, Carolinians, frontiersmen, and farmers. But we are one army now, bound by the same purpose."

A murmur of assent passed through the men.

"We march not because it is easy, or certain, but because no one else will. If Ferguson crosses these mountains unchallenged, he'll burn every homestead between here and the Nolichucky. And he'll do it flying the King's banner."

Elias looked around. The men were listening—really listening. Even the skeptics had grown still.

"We may not agree on every step," Campbell continued, glancing at Shelby and Sevier, "but we march together. Because the alternative is to kneel. And

I've yet to meet a man here who came to kneel."

A cheer broke the tension like a thunderclap. It was ragged at first, but it spread—stronger, louder, defiant. Elias felt it rise in his chest like a flame. For a moment, the fear melted away.

They were not soldiers. But they were not alone.

And they were not backing down.

Dawn arrived with mist and mud. Elias trudged alongside the column, boots heavy from the damp, his musket slung across his back and a sack of smoked meat weighing against his hip. They had made better time after Campbell's speech. It hadn't solved all their problems, but it had reminded the men of something vital—that their strength came not from polished boots or drilled lines, but from the grit and resolve of men with no one else to depend on.

That morning, they approached the Watauga River—a churning, swollen ribbon of water that sliced through the dense forest like a blade. It had rained in the night, and the banks had overrun with a vengeance. What was a manageable ford two days earlier was now a muddy, boiling torrent.

Elias stood at the edge and watched a branch get swallowed whole by the current. He looked to Caleb. "We're not crossing that, are we?"

Caleb gave a grim nod. "We don't have much choice."

Word spread quickly that the main force would begin constructing rafts and finding a safe place to ferry over supplies. Horses were led upstream to shallower ground. Wagons were unloaded. Men who'd once swung axes in forests now turned them to trees with purpose, felling trunks and lashing them with rawhide and hemp.

Elias worked beside a boy not much older than himself, a redheaded farmhand named Micah from over the ridge in Burke County. Together they stripped bark and helped wedge the logs into rough frames. The water roared nearby, loud enough to muffle conversation.

"You ever done this before?" Elias shouted over the din.

Micah shook his head. "Nope. Closest I've come to crossing a river was floating a pig carcass down the creek to confuse the taxman."

Elias stared at him. "That worked?"

Micah grinned. "Only for a day. The fool followed the smell and found the rest of the hog buried behind my ma's chicken coop."

They both laughed—true, unguarded laughter. It felt strange, like the return of something long buried.

By midday, the rafts were ready, and the crossing began.

The first went over carrying a half-dozen men and their gear. The current fought them the whole way, tugging the raft downstream with the hunger of a wild dog. Elias and Caleb were on the third trip, along with two others and several crates of powder and lead.

As they pushed off, Elias knelt low, clutching the sides as the raft bucked and wobbled. The cold spray slapped his face, and he tasted the silt in his mouth. Caleb took the pole at the front, shouting orders to counterbalance the load as they veered hard left. One misstep, one snapped rope, and they'd be dragged under.

The far bank approached fast—too fast.

"Brace!" Caleb yelled.

They struck mud with a bone-jarring jolt, the raft tilting wildly before slamming flat. Elias tumbled forward but caught himself on the edge. They scrambled ashore, soaked and shivering, but alive.

Once across, Elias turned to watch the others begin the process again. It would take the rest of the day to get everyone over—maybe longer. Still, spirits rose. Each successful crossing brought more cheers, more laughter. Even the most sour-faced Loyalist-turned-Patriot cracked a grin as the horses splashed across.

But the weather turned by evening.

Dark clouds rolled in from the east, and the wind picked up with a whistle through the trees. By the time the last raft pushed off, rain had begun to fall again—first in fat drops, then in torrents. Thunder rolled in the distance.

Those already across scrambled to cover the crates and supplies with oiled canvas. A few dug shallow trenches around the camp to keep runoff from pooling in the center. Fires sputtered in the wind, casting flickering halos over soaked shoulders.

Elias and Caleb shared a lean-to with two others—Reuben, a long-faced tanner, and Daniel, a quiet Quaker who carried no weapon but tended wounds with a healer's hands. Their shelter leaned hard against a stump, tarped with canvas and lashed with vines.

Inside, the four huddled together, steam rising from their damp coats.

"You think we'll catch Ferguson in time?" Elias asked no one in particular.

Reuben spat into the mud. "If we don't, then we better hope he don't catch us first."

Daniel said nothing, just listened to the rain, his hands clasped in silent prayer.

That night, thunder cracked above the canopy like cannon fire. Elias couldn't sleep. Every gust of wind reminded him how close they were to being scattered by forces they couldn't control—nature, time, and war. But he wasn't alone. He clung to that.

In the morning, the rain eased to a drizzle. The camp emerged slowly from its cocoon of misery, men stomping their boots and shaking out their cloaks. Despite the exhaustion, the crossing had changed something. A shared trial— one more stitch in the patchwork of brotherhood that had begun to bind the Overmountain Men together.

But not all was mended.

As the wagons were repacked, word came that another scouting party had found signs of Loyalist movement to the southeast. Ferguson's campfires had been spotted near Cowpens—too close for comfort. The commanders convened again under the grey sky, and decisions were made quickly.

"We ride hard from here," Shelby declared. "No more delays."

"We lighten the load," Sevier added. "Anything not vital stays behind."

That sparked protest.

"Leave our food behind?" a man cried.

"Abandon the extra powder?"

"You'll be marching us to death!"

Colonel Campbell stepped forward. "We march for one battle. One. Every ounce of weight we spare is one more hour gained."

A hard silence fell.

In the end, they left behind what they could: extra blankets, cooking pots, even spare boots. Elias kept only what he needed—his musket, a pouch of powder and shot, a knife, and a bundle of dried meat. He wrapped his few possessions in oilcloth and slung them tight.

By midday, they were moving again. Faster. Harder.

The trees thinned into open ridges, and the air shifted—less of the wet mountain cold and more of the dry rustle of falling leaves. Elias could feel the distance closing. They were crossing from retreat into pursuit. From waiting into confrontation.

He rode part of the way beside Rebecca, who had taken up the reins of a borrowed mare, her rifle across her back. Her expression was unreadable— calm, determined, with none of the hesitation some of the men wore.

"You ride like you've done this before," Elias said.

She smiled faintly. "I've had practice chasing stubborn livestock through worse."

They crested a low hill, and the valley beyond opened wide. Far on the horizon, a faint plume of smoke drifted skyward. Ferguson? Or another farm?

No one knew.

But they were closing in.

And this time, there would be no turning back.

The ridge trail narrowed, forcing the Overmountain column into single file. Loose shale crunched underfoot, and the wind carried scents of pine, smoke, and something darker—burnt grain or scorched wood. Elias clutched his musket tighter. The sun slanted low across the hills now, its light filtered through a veil of dust and haze. Every crow's call echoed louder than it should have. Even the seasoned frontiersmen rode quieter.

Rumors passed through the column like wildfire.

"Ferguson's not far."

"He's raiding farms, torching barns."

"He left a warning nailed to a door—said he'd hang every rebel that crossed the ridge."

Elias tried not to dwell on it. But the way men gripped their weapons, the way they glanced over their shoulders—it was clear. The chase was no longer theoretical. It was real, and it was closing fast.

A rider galloped down the line, splattered with mud and urgency.

"Burned homestead two miles back," he shouted to the officers. "Still smoking. No survivors."

A growl of rage rippled through the men. Elias saw Thomas McBride, one of the older volunteers from Greene County, slam his fist into a tree trunk as he passed it. His own son had stayed behind to protect their home.

They rode faster after that.

Caleb broke the silence beside Elias. "You see the smoke last night?"

Elias nodded. "It wasn't just from campfires."

"Ferguson's playing with fire. Trying to scare us off."

"Do you think he'll stand and fight?"

Caleb's face was a storm cloud. "He will. Pride like his doesn't run."

By noon, they passed the charred remains of a farmhouse—its roof collapsed, walls blackened. The stink of ash and something else—sickly sweet—hung in the air. No bodies, just silence and smoldering ruin. A woman's shoe lay in the yard, small and brown, scorched at the heel.

No one spoke.

The column pressed on.

That evening, they camped at the edge of a thicket near Cowpens, the site of an old pasture where Whigs and Loyalists had once bartered cattle under truce. Now, it was a no-man's-land.

The officers called a quiet council.

Elias lingered on the outskirts, close enough to catch fragments of their voices. Colonel Campbell stood with his arms folded tight, while Sevier jabbed the dirt with a stick as he spoke. Shelby watched the eastern hills, silent until finally stepping forward.

"We engage him soon," he said. "He's either cornered, or he wants us to think he is. Either way, we don't wait."

Some officers murmured approval. A few looked uneasy.

Sevier added, "Tomorrow, we move before dawn. We strike before he expects us."

"Will he expect a night approach?" someone asked.

"No," said Shelby. "He thinks we're tired. And he's right."

But Elias, sitting beside the fire with his blanket pulled over his shoulders, noticed something else—resolve. They were tired. Exhausted. But a fire had been lit in them. This wasn't a defensive war anymore. They were taking the fight to Ferguson.

Later that night, Elias and Caleb sat near the fire while Rebecca checked her flintlock. The tension in the camp had changed. It wasn't just fear anymore—it was the quiet before a storm.

Elias turned to her. "You've seen the way Ferguson works."

She nodded. "I saw what was left behind when he came through Wofford's Iron Works. Scorched earth. He wants to crush us before we gather."

"Why hasn't he fled east?" Caleb asked.

"Because he thinks we won't make it this far," she said. "Or maybe he wants the fight. He's got British regulars now, and plenty of Loyalist militia."

Elias swallowed. "Do we stand a chance?"

Rebecca locked eyes with him. "Only if we move faster than he thinks possible."

Before first light, the Overmountain Men were already marching.

The stars still hung low in the western sky as boots crunched through wet leaves and frost-bitten grass. Torches were banned—no firelight to give away their movement. They moved in darkness, guided by scouts and memory, riding low through valleys and shadowed woods.

Elias walked beside Caleb, his breath pluming in the cold, the rhythm of their steps like a drumbeat. Even the horses seemed subdued, sensing the gravity of what lay ahead.

As dawn broke pale across the ridgeline, they reached a small rise overlooking a valley below—rolling land, wooded ridges, and a clearing in the center where campfires glowed.

There—like ants clustered around embers—was Ferguson's camp.

Elias dropped to his stomach in the brush, heart pounding. So this was it. The British flag fluttered above a cluster of tents. Men moved in the early light, dragging firewood, tending to horses. They didn't know what was coming.

Caleb crouched beside him, whispering. "We're close. Closer than I expected."

Down below, Ferguson's men looked at ease—confident, maybe even careless. They believed they had days to prepare. Maybe they did yesterday.

But not today.

Orders rippled through the Overmountain ranks. Colonel Campbell's voice was low but charged with purpose. "We surround the hill. Three columns. We strike from every side. No mercy."

Elias took a deep breath. He thought of his father, of Samuel, of their forge on the slope of Buffalo Mountain. He thought of the way his mother's hands smelled like iron and lavender.

This was why he'd come.

He wasn't just a boy anymore. He was here for them.

As he loaded his musket, his fingers trembled—not with fear, but with a fevered anticipation.

They would strike soon.

But before the command was given, a single shot rang out from down the hill—a warning or an accident, no one knew.

Then all at once, chaos.

The woods exploded with thunder.

That first musket shot—whoever fired it—was answered at once by a storm of return fire from the Overmountain Men. The crack of rifles echoed down the ridge like God Himself had shattered the sky. Elias flinched as the sound hit him, loud as the forge bell in his father's shop, but sharper—more violent, more real. The waiting was over.

He gripped his musket tight and charged forward with Caleb at his side, both of them pushing through the underbrush that tangled around their boots. Leaves slapped against Elias's face. The air smelled of smoke and mud and something metallic, something raw. Gunfire barked from the slope above, muzzle flashes blooming like fireflies in a storm. Ferguson's Loyalists were awake now—rattled, but fighting back.

"Move! Now!" Caleb yelled over the din.

Elias didn't need the encouragement. He was already running, crouched low, weaving between trees, heart pounding in his throat. All around them, men surged forward—neighbors and farmers, hunters and tanners, preachers and blacksmiths, all turned soldiers in a single breath. Their homemade powder horns rattled. Their buckskins were streaked with sweat and dirt. And still they advanced.

He reached a wide pine and knelt behind it, trying to breathe. Caleb dropped beside him, reloading with practiced speed. Elias's hands fumbled—powder, patch, ball, ramrod. He had drilled the motions a hundred times, but never like this. His hands were slick. The barrel shook.

Then he raised the musket, sighted downhill through the smoke, and pulled the trigger.

The recoil slammed into his shoulder like a blacksmith's hammer. He didn't see if the shot landed. A figure in a red coat staggered back, then dropped from sight.

Reload. Again.

Shelby's men pressed from the west, Sevier's from the east, Campbell's straight up the center. They weren't fighting in lines, not like the British. They fought from tree to tree, boulder to boulder, musket shots coming from hidden spots like the forest itself had turned on the enemy. They were wolves in the woods.

A voice cried out ahead—one of Ferguson's officers on horseback, sabre flashing as he tried to rally a line. "Hold! Hold the ridge!"

Rebecca's rifle cracked. The officer toppled from his horse, tumbling end over end into the ferns below. She ducked back behind a log, her face calm, deadly.

"They're breaking," she called to Elias and Caleb. "Don't let up."

The slope was chaos. Loyalist soldiers fell back toward the crest, slipping over rocks slick with dew—and blood. Their formation was a mess, a twisting knot of men trying to reload, to fire, to run. But the rebels kept coming.

Elias charged uphill again, the ground uneven and treacherous. His legs burned. His shoulder throbbed. Another musket ball whined past his ear like a wasp. He dropped flat, belly scraping over gravel. He heard someone shouting for a medic—then another voice screaming for God.

There was no room for fear anymore. Only motion.

He reached a clump of laurel bushes where Caleb crouched, bleeding from a shallow gash along his temple.

"You alright?" Elias asked.

Caleb nodded, panting. "I'll live. Reload. We're not done."

From their spot, Elias could see the top of the ridge now. Ferguson's command post was perched near the summit—a small rocky rise with a broken fence and a scattering of tents. And there—standing tall in a gray coat streaked with powder—was Ferguson himself.

He sat high on a white horse, blowing a silver whistle that shrilled above the battle. Even in the chaos, he looked composed, determined. He swung his saber like a conductor leading a bloody orchestra, directing his scattered men to new firing lines.

"That's him," Elias whispered.

Caleb nodded. "We get up there, this ends."

Rebels to the north screamed a battle cry, and a wave of men stormed up the incline. Ferguson's defenders fired point-blank into them—three men fell, rolling backward down the slope. But the rest surged on.

Elias scrambled forward. He reached a fallen tree and used it for cover, bracing his musket and aiming toward the command post. It was too far for an accurate shot. Still, he fired.

The smoke rolled thick now, curling between the trees like fog in a graveyard. The sound of musketry merged into a deafening roar—no gaps, no silences, just the endless hammering of war. Someone behind Elias let out a ragged yell. Then another voice cried, "Bayonets! Up the center!"

He turned. Sevier's men were fixing blades and charging in a wedge up the slope, howling like demons. The defenders at the top faltered, some breaking ranks, others firing one last volley before fleeing.

Elias couldn't look away. The sight of it—the rage and momentum, the sheer refusal to stop—it burned itself into him.

Then Ferguson moved.

He spurred his horse and wheeled toward the rear, trying to escape the ring tightening around him. He blew his whistle again, trying to rally a final defense. "Push them back! Hold this ground!"

But the ground would not be held.

A volley cracked from the left flank—one shot, then three more in quick succession. Ferguson jerked in the saddle. A red flower bloomed on his chest. He slumped, but didn't fall. Another shot rang out. His horse reared. Ferguson pitched sideways, tumbling to the earth.

The whistle tumbled from his hand and landed in the dirt.

For a second, time seemed to pause.

Then it collapsed.

With their commander fallen, the Loyalists broke. Some ran. Some surrendered. Some threw down their rifles and sank to their knees. The fight drained from them like water from a pierced barrel.

"Cease fire!" Campbell shouted from the ridge's edge. "Cease fire, for the Lord's sake!"

But not everyone heard. A few more shots cracked—one man fell, hands raised, eyes wide. Another was shot in the back trying to run. Officers dashed between units, waving arms, shouting for calm.

Elias stumbled forward, dazed. His ears rang. His shirt was soaked with sweat. Around him, the battlefield lay in ruin.

Men wept. Men screamed. Some stood still as statues.

Rebecca walked past him, rifle lowered, her eyes hard. "It's over."

He looked down at his hands—black with powder, trembling slightly.

It was over.

They buried Ferguson on the hill where he died.

His body was riddled with musket wounds—seven by some counts, eight by others. His gray coat was soaked in blood. They stripped him of his insignia, his whistle, and his saber before the burial.

"He came into our hills to burn us out," Shelby said, his voice flat. "Now he'll stay here forever."

No one argued.

The white horse wandered the slope alone now, untethered. It trotted through the grass, sniffing at fallen men with twitching ears. Elias watched it for a long time, struck by its gentleness amid the carnage. The animal didn't know it had carried death.

Later, the men gathered for roll call. The names read aloud were punctuated by silence. Too many had no answer. Samuel wasn't one of them—he hadn't been here—but Elias felt his brother's ghost beside him all the same. Watching. Measuring.

Caleb sat near the fire, head in hands. Rebecca stared into the flames, eyes distant.

Elias stood alone at the edge of the ridge, staring down into the valley where the battle had begun.

He had crossed the mountains to fight tyranny. He had faced the thunder. And he had lived.

But something had changed.

The boy who left home with a borrowed rifle and his brother's ring was not the one standing here now. This boy had killed. Had bled. Had seen what men became when pushed too far.

He felt no pride. No glory.

Only gravity.

And the wind across the ridge carried a truth he could not escape: the war wasn't over.

This was only the beginning.

Chapter 4

The morning after the battle dawned gray, the clouds hanging low like a shroud over the ridge. The smell of smoke still clung to the trees, and the earth was churned and bloodied where the fight had raged. Elias awoke on the cold ground, stiff and sore, muscles tight from the strain of battle and sleep stolen in fragments.

All around him, the Overmountain camp had taken on a solemn quiet. Men moved with the heaviness of the wounded—some physically, some only in the soul. A few fires still smoldered from the night before, but there was no song, no talk of glory. There was only the slow, methodical work of reckoning.

Elias stood and stretched, then wandered toward the place where the bodies had been gathered. There were dozens—some wrapped in canvas, others laid bare, eyes frozen in terror or peace or pain. Rebel and Loyalist alike. The battlefield hadn't cared who they were.

He found Caleb near the edge of the slope, digging with a crude spade beside a group of other men. Dirt clung to his boots and forearms. His face was hollow, streaked with sweat and dried blood.

"Morning," Elias said, voice hoarse.

Caleb didn't look up. "Grab a shovel."

They worked without speaking for a while. Each time Elias drove the blade into the soil, he felt it jar through his shoulders and down his spine. They were digging graves—row after row, shallow but decent. Some of the men muttered prayers as they worked. Others wept quietly.

A few paces away, Rebecca knelt beside a young Loyalist no older than sixteen. His chest was riddled with shot, but his face looked almost peaceful, like he might've been sleeping if not for the blood. She placed a pine bough over his face, then rose and walked toward the next.

"How many?" Elias asked Caleb finally.

Caleb wiped his brow. "More than a hundred Loyalists. Around thirty of ours."

Elias swallowed. "Too many."

Caleb gave a grim nod. "We won. But it doesn't feel like it, does it?"

Elias didn't answer. He just kept digging.

Hours passed like that—digging, carrying, laying to rest. No one told them to do it. It was the kind of work that had to be done, and they knew it. Shelby himself helped carry the body of a fallen scout. Campbell stood with a small group of Virginia men, reading Psalms over their comrades.

Even the sky seemed to mourn. Rain began to fall in a fine mist by midmorning, turning the dirt to thick clay. Elias's hands blistered, but he didn't stop. With each grave, the weight in his chest pressed heavier.

At last, they came to bury Ferguson.

His body lay beneath a makeshift canopy, draped in a rough wool blanket. The blood had dried into his coat, and his face had taken on a strange calm. One of the older men tossed Ferguson's broken whistle onto his chest.

Shelby stood over him and muttered, "He thought he'd break us."

A few of the men spat on the ground. Others turned away. Rebecca stood beside Elias, silent. "He came here to burn us," she said. "Now the mountain's taken him instead."

Elias studied the dead commander. He wasn't much older than some of their own leaders. And yet here he lay—stripped of power, of command, of voice. Just another man in the dirt.

"What'll they say about him?" Elias asked.

"That depends on who's doing the telling," Caleb replied.

They buried Ferguson without ceremony, in a shallow grave a few yards from the ridge's crest. Some said it was too much honor. Others said it was just. No one argued long. They were too tired.

By midday, the worst of the work was done. Fires were stoked. Meat was cooked. Elias sat beneath a tree and tried to clean the grime from under his nails. His stomach churned when he looked down at the streaks of blood on his shirt.

Rebecca sat nearby, sharpening her blade with a small whetstone. The rhythm of it—scrape, scrape, scrape—was strangely comforting.

"You alright?" she asked.

Elias hesitated. "I don't know. I thought I would feel something different. Pride, maybe. Or relief."

"And what do you feel?"

He stared out at the ridge where the battle had raged just the day before. "Like something's been torn open. And I'm not sure if it'll ever close again."

Rebecca nodded. "It's like that. The first time. You never forget it."

"Will it get easier?"

"No," she said. "But you'll get stronger. If you don't let it break you."

They sat in silence for a while. The mist had lifted, but the clouds remained. Somewhere to the north, a hawk circled lazily in the gray sky.

Later, Elias joined the others in tending to the wounded. He bound Caleb's gash with clean cloth. He helped carry a man with a shattered leg to a makeshift tent where a preacher-turned-surgeon worked with trembling hands. The cries of pain were sharp and sudden, but quieter now than they had been.

Toward evening, he wandered back to where the graves had been dug. Most were already covered, simple wooden crosses marking names where they could. One cross bore no name, just the initials *W.M.*—carved in shaky strokes.

Elias knelt beside that one.

He thought of his brother. Of the trail that had brought him here. Of the blood on his hands and the thunder in his ears.

He wasn't a boy anymore. He didn't know what he was, exactly. But he knew he would never be the same.

Behind him, the camp was quiet. The Overmountain Men had done what they came to do. The battle was won.

But the war still waited.

And somewhere beyond the hills, the world turned.

The day after the burials, the mountain took on a different mood—quieter, but tense. There was no more weeping or ceremony. Just murmurs, watchful eyes, and the heavy question that hung between every campfire and mess line: What do we do with the prisoners?

Nearly 700 Loyalists had surrendered at the end of the battle, many of them Tennesseans, Carolinians, even some from over the mountain. Some were boys barely old enough to carry a musket. Others had been militia, not hardened Tories. Still others had killed neighbors, burned barns, or worse. The lines weren't so easy to draw.

A small field near the ridge had been cordoned off, the prisoners kept under constant watch. Armed sentries paced the perimeter, eyes hard and muskets loaded. The Loyalists sat on the cold ground, huddled together, waiting.

That morning, Shelby, Campbell, and Sevier met in a small circle of officers just beyond the prisoner camp. Elias watched from a distance as they argued, their voices low but sharp. The question was justice. Or vengeance.

"That man there—he's the one who burned the Taylor farm!" one of the militiamen cried later, pointing a finger at a squat, red-faced Loyalist near the front of the camp. "He shot Mr. Taylor dead on his porch!"

A chorus of angry voices followed, some shouting, others pleading. Shelby raised a hand for silence.

"We are not butchers," he said, loud enough to carry. "But we are not blind, either. There will be trials. Proper ones. And punishment for those who deserve it."

Sevier stepped forward, nodding grimly. "We'll form a tribunal of officers. We'll listen to witness accounts. And the men proven guilty of war crimes—of murder, rape, or burning civilians—they'll hang."

The word settled over the camp like a storm cloud.

Elias swallowed hard. It was the right thing. But it was also the thing he dreaded most.

That afternoon, the trials began.

They set up a makeshift court beneath a canvas awning near the center of the ridge. Three chairs were placed at a table—Shelby, Sevier, and Campbell presiding. Witnesses came forward—farmers, scouts, wives of the dead. Some were calm. Some shouted through tears. But all spoke of the horrors they had endured.

Elias sat on a log a few yards away, watching in silence. Caleb stood beside him, arms crossed.

"You believe in all this?" Elias asked. "The trials?"

Caleb nodded slowly. "Better than slaughter. Truth is, it'd be easier to hang them all. But that'd make us no better than Ferguson."

One by one, the prisoners were called forward. Some denied everything. Others broke down and confessed. One man—Harold Watts, a Loyalist from Rowan County—was found guilty of setting fire to a homestead with a family inside. A woman in the crowd screamed when she saw him. He was sentenced to hang.

When the time came, a rope was thrown over a sturdy branch, and a small crowd gathered in grim silence. Elias watched from behind a tree, heart thudding. Watts didn't resist. He climbed the barrel on shaking legs, weeping. No one said a prayer. No one cheered. The rope tightened, the barrel fell, and it was done.

Elias turned away and retched behind a tree.

"You alright?" Rebecca asked quietly. She had approached without sound, arms folded.

"I don't know," he said, wiping his mouth. "Feels like we just won a war, and now we're killing men all over again."

Rebecca looked out at the ridge. "War doesn't end when the shooting stops. Sometimes it just changes shape."

He nodded, the weight pressing down again.

By the third day, five more had been tried and sentenced. Two were hanged, three imprisoned under guard until they could be transferred. The men tried to be fair, but fairness was a shifting thing on a battlefield. Elias could see it in their faces—that tired, hollow look of men trying to carry justice like a burden.

Some in the camp grew restless.

"They killed our kin," one man spat. "Burned our barns. I say let 'em swing."

Others—older men mostly—argued for mercy. "We've made our point. No need for more blood."

Shelby addressed the camp that evening. "We came here to break Ferguson's hold on the mountain. We did that. But if we become what he was, then we've lost more than we know."

That night, Elias lay awake, staring up at the stars. The ridge had grown quiet again. But it was the uneasy quiet of a storm passed—not peace.

He thought of Samuel. Of what his brother would've done if he'd been here. Would Samuel have voted to hang them?

Would he have stood with the tribunal, or the men crying out for vengeance?

Elias didn't know. The war had taken Samuel before such questions could be answered.

But the echoes of it—of justice and judgment, of blood and mercy—reverberated still.

The next morning, the last of the trials were concluded. A handful of prisoners remained, to be taken back across the mountains for safekeeping. Others would be released with warnings, marked men in a divided land.

Campbell gave the order to strike the tribunal awning.

Shelby watched as the final rope was cut down from the tree.

And Elias, standing nearby, couldn't shake the thought that no matter how high the mountain or how just the cause, war left no one untouched.

The Overmountain camp slowly began to dissolve after the trials ended. Word had come from the governors of North Carolina and Virginia: the victory at Kings Mountain had struck a critical blow. Ferguson's death had thrown Cornwallis' plans into disarray. The tide, for the first time in a long time, seemed to be turning.

Yet no one in camp seemed particularly triumphant.

The men busied themselves packing supplies, burying scraps of gear too damaged to carry, and preparing for the long ride home. The fires burned lower now. Voices were quieter. And Elias felt something inside him go quiet, too.

He stood alone at the ridge's edge, overlooking the battlefield once more.

The grass was scorched where musket balls had struck. Bits of uniform still clung to broken twigs. The ground was muddied and scattered with the long-dead leaves of early autumn.

He crouched and ran a hand through the soil. A musket ball surfaced in his palm. It was dark and battered, cold from the earth.

"Seems smaller than it did that day," he muttered to himself.

"Funny how that happens," said a voice behind him.

Elias turned to see Rebecca approaching. She wore a light wool cloak against the chill, her braid tied back, her rifle slung over one shoulder. Her boots crunched quietly against the damp leaves as she stopped beside him.

"You been out here long?" she asked.

Elias nodded. "Just thinking. Trying to understand what this all means."

Rebecca tilted her head. "And?"

"I don't know. I thought killing Ferguson would fix everything. That winning the battle would make us feel... safe. Proud, even."

She crossed her arms, face turned toward the tree line.

"Safe?" she repeated. "Maybe. But proud? That comes and goes."

"I keep seeing their faces," Elias said softly. "Not just the ones we buried. The ones we tried. The ones we hanged."

Rebecca looked at him, eyes sharp but not unkind.

"You think you did wrong?"

"I don't know," Elias admitted. "I think we had to. But it doesn't feel right. Not the way stories say it should."

Rebecca let that hang in the air for a while. Then she sat on a rock and gestured for Elias to join her.

"My father used to say the truth of war is always muddy," she began. "Said you don't ever get to walk away clean. Just with fewer stains than the other side."

Elias sank down beside her, gripping the musket ball.

"I used to think about war like it was some kind of proving ground," he said. "Like if I could fight, I'd be like Samuel. Brave. Strong."

"You don't think you were brave?" she asked.

He looked down. "Not the way he was. Not without wondering every step if

I belonged here."

Rebecca was quiet for a long moment. Then she reached over and took the musket ball from his hand.

"You don't have to be Samuel," she said. "You're not meant to be. You're Elias. And what you did here—facing men trying to kill you, holding the line when others fell, choosing justice over rage—that takes a different kind of strength."

Elias blinked, unsure how to respond. Her words settled into him like water into dry earth—quiet, but necessary.

"You could've turned back before the ridge," she added. "You didn't."

"I thought about it," he admitted.

"We all did."

A silence passed between them, filled only by the wind rustling through the trees. Down below, a small detail of men were tending to the last of the supply wagons.

"You heading home soon?" she asked.

Elias shrugged. "I guess. But it feels like I'm not the same boy who left."

"You're not," Rebecca said. "That's the point."

He looked over at her. "And you? What happens next?"

She smiled faintly. "I'll return to Watauga. Help rebuild. Help folks find what pieces they can. Maybe I'll keep my rifle close for a while, just in case."

He nodded.

"Maybe I'll visit," he said before he could think better of it.

Rebecca turned toward him with a small grin. "You'd better."

They shared a brief look—awkward, tentative, warm—and then she rose.

"Come on. Help me with this last load. The sooner we're packed, the sooner we start home."

They walked together back toward the main camp.

Later that evening, Elias found himself by the fire beside Caleb, Josiah, and a few others from the company. They sat in a circle, sipping watered-down whiskey, staring into the flames.

"Reckon they'll write about us?" Caleb said suddenly.

Josiah snorted. "Doubt it. We ain't fancy enough. No uniforms, no polished boots."

Caleb leaned back. "Still. Somebody might. 'The Men from Over the Mountain.' Has a nice ring to it."

"More likely they'll write about Ferguson," Josiah replied. "Or about Shelby, Sevier, and Campbell. Not a bunch of half-starved, smoke-covered boys like us."

Elias said nothing. He stared into the fire, remembering the faces, the sounds, the stillness after the thunder. He hoped someone would write about it one day. Not just the battle, but the burden of surviving it.

Eventually, the fire died low. The men slipped off to bed, one by one. Elias lingered, letting the cold night wrap around him.

He reached into his coat pocket and felt the musket ball again. It had cooled, but it still felt heavy.

From across the dark, the voice of Reverend Dooley rose in soft prayer. No fire lit his face, but Elias knew the preacher knelt somewhere near the edge of the sleeping camp, whispering to the God they'd all cried out to during the thunder.

"Let us remember the fallen," Dooley murmured. "And let us never forget the price of freedom."

Elias closed his eyes.

He thought of home. Of his father's forge. Of Samuel's grave. Of all the lives turned like leaves by this war.

He had set out to find strength. What he had found was truth.

And with the truth came weight—and the first glimmer of understanding.

The morning after the trials dawned cool and bright, a fragile promise of calm after the storm. The camp was restless, packed with men eager to move, yet hesitant to leave the place where so much had been lost and won. Horses whinnied softly, saddles creaked, and the sound of muskets being cleaned punctuated the crisp mountain air.

Elias stood among the others, his hands busy securing his worn leather satchel, but his thoughts heavy. The battle, the justice, the faces of those lost—they all weighed on him like a thick fog. Around him, familiar voices rose and fell, but he felt distant, caught in his own reflections.

Caleb approached with a hearty slap on Elias's shoulder. "Ready to ride, boy? We've got a long road ahead."

Elias nodded, managing a small smile. "As ready as I'll ever be."

The column formed slowly, horses lined up, packs strapped tight, and the captives still held under watch. The ride home would be grueling—steep, winding paths through forests thick with leaf and shadow, but the thought of returning to familiar soil sparked a flicker of hope in Elias's chest.

As they set off, the mountain air filled with the rhythm of hooves and soft conversation. Some men sang quiet songs, others fell into brooding silence. Elias found himself riding beside Rebecca, her expression thoughtful as she glanced sideways at him.

"You alright?" she asked quietly.

Elias took a breath. "I think so. Just... everything feels different now."

Rebecca nodded knowingly. "It does. You're not the boy who left."

He remembered her words from the night before and gave a small chuckle. "No, I'm not."

The trail wound down through the dense trees, the sunlight dappling the forest floor. The scent of pine and earth was sharp and clear. Elias found comfort in the familiar smells, but the landscape seemed forever changed, marked by the scars of war.

As the miles passed, the camp slowed. The men became quieter, their energy sapped not just by the ride but by the weight of what they'd done and seen. Elias noticed more than a few men nursing bruised limbs or limp horses, the wounds of battle and hardship still fresh.

At a clearing near a creek, the column stopped to rest. Men dismounted, and the horses drank deeply. Fires were lit, and the smell of cooking meat mingled with the fresh water.

Elias sat on a fallen log, watching the ripples in the creek. He thought about home—about the blacksmith's shop, his father's steady hands shaping iron, the warmth of the forge's fire. He missed it terribly, though he wasn't sure if the boy who had left would ever truly return.

Rebecca joined him silently, holding a tin cup of water.

"Samuel's grave," she said suddenly. "Will you visit?"

Elias swallowed hard. "I want to. I have to. It's the least I can do."

She nodded, her eyes soft with understanding. "He's a good man. And he'd be proud of you."

The words brought a warmth to Elias's chest he hadn't expected. He looked away, brushing a stray lock of hair from his forehead.

"We all have things we carry," Rebecca continued. "Some are wounds. Others are memories. Some are hopes."

Elias gazed into the woods, feeling the weight of those words settle inside him.

The camp eventually packed again, the column moving deeper into the mountains. The terrain grew rugged and steep, the path sometimes little more than a narrow trail between towering trees. Elias held tight to his horse's reins, focusing on the path ahead to keep his thoughts at bay.

As night fell, they made camp beneath a canopy of stars, the sky vast and silent above them. The men gathered around fires, sharing stories in low voices, laughter breaking through the tension now and then.

Elias sat close to the fire, the flickering flames casting shadows across his face. He thought about the men who had died, the friends who had fallen beside him, the justice they had tried to uphold. The war had changed everything— his family, his home, his very sense of who he was.

He wondered if he would ever find peace.

Later, as the camp settled into silence, Elias found himself walking to the edge of the woods. The moon hung high, pale and steady. He knelt by a small patch of wildflowers, the same kind his mother had once planted in their garden.

"Samuel," he whispered, voice catching. "I'm coming home. And I'll carry you with me."

The night held its quiet vigil as Elias stood, a boy changed by fire and loss, moving toward the uncertain dawn.

The journey home stretched before them like a long, winding river, full of both promise and uncertainty. Each mile carried Elias farther from the battles he had fought and closer to the life he had once known — though that life felt distant now, like a half-remembered dream.

The sun was high as the company broke camp early, eager to press onward through the thick woods. The air smelled of damp leaves and fresh pine, but beneath the pleasant scents was the persistent ache of fatigue and the subtle tension of unfinished business.

Elias rode beside Caleb once more, who hummed a quiet tune to keep his spirits up.

"Feels strange to be heading back after all that's happened," Caleb said, shading his eyes against the sun.

"Yeah," Elias agreed, glancing at the trees racing past. "I'm not sure what to expect when we get home."

Caleb gave him a knowing look. "Neither am I. Things don't just go back to how they were before a fight like that."

They rode in thoughtful silence until a sudden shout from the front startled the men into alertness. Word spread quickly: a small band of settlers was spotted ahead, waving and calling.

As the riders approached, Elias recognized familiar faces — neighbors from the valley, families who had stayed behind during the fighting. Relief washed over him in a wave. There were smiles, tears, and embraces as the reunited friends shared news and hope.

Among them was old Mr. Whitaker, a grizzled farmer who had been like a grandfather to Elias during his childhood.

"Thank God you're all safe!" Whitaker exclaimed, gripping Elias's shoulder. "Heard the news of the battle — Kings Mountain, they call it. You boys did us proud."

Elias smiled but felt a pang of sorrow beneath the joy. "It came at a cost," he said quietly.

Whitaker nodded, eyes softening. "A heavy cost, but freedom never comes easy."

As they shared stories, Elias's heart stirred with a new sense of purpose. This land, these people, were worth fighting for — worth rebuilding.

The men traded news of what had happened in the surrounding settlements while Elias listened, drinking in every detail. Some spoke of neighbors lost to raids or disease; others spoke of hope as families prepared to return to their farms. The world beyond the battlefield was changing, and Elias felt the pull of it stronger than ever.

That evening, Elias returned to his family's farm. The familiar creak of the porch steps, the scent of wood smoke curling from the chimney, brought a bittersweet ache. His father was waiting, older now, his hands rough and calloused from years at the forge.

"Elias," his father said, voice thick with emotion. "You came back."

Elias nodded, swallowing the lump in his throat. "I did. And I've seen things no boy should have to see."

His father pulled him into a strong embrace. "But you came through. That makes a man. Your brother Samuel would be proud."

The mention of Samuel made Elias's eyes sting, but he held himself steady.

Later, in the quiet of his old room, Elias sat by the fading firelight, the musket ball he had carried still heavy in his pocket. He thought about the journey — the battles, the justice, the sacrifices — and the path ahead.

It would not be easy. The war was far from over, and the land bore scars that time alone could not heal.

But for the first time since he had left, Elias felt a spark of hope. A promise that, despite the darkness, new beginnings were possible.

He was ready to face whatever came next.

The days that followed were filled with both comfort and challenge. Elias worked alongside his father in the forge, the familiar clang of hammer on anvil grounding him as he relearned the rhythms of home. The forge's heat was both a balm and a reminder — the fire that shaped iron also shaped him, forging a new resolve.

He spent mornings helping in the fields, mending fences, and repairing what the war had torn apart. The soil was stubborn and dry in places, but the land still held its promise. Each seed planted was a small act of faith.

Neighbors stopped by often, bringing news, food, and stories of survival. They spoke in hushed tones about the uncertain future, the shifting alliances, and the ever-present threat of more conflict. Yet beneath the worry was a shared determination to rebuild and protect their homes.

Elias found himself drawn to the younger children in the village, telling them stories of bravery and hope, trying to keep their spirits alive. He taught some to shoot a musket, others to track animals in the woods. These moments of joy were fragile but precious.

One afternoon, as the sun dipped low, Elias took a walk to the small graveyard where Samuel was buried. The wooden marker, simple and weathered, stood among wildflowers swaying in the breeze. Elias knelt, tracing the carved letters with a rough finger.

"I wish you were here," he whispered. "I'm trying to be the man you believed I could be."

He placed a smooth stone on the grave, a silent promise to carry his brother's memory forward.

The wind rustled through the trees, carrying the faint scent of pine and earth, as if the mountain itself was listening.

But peace was fragile. Rumors of unrest stirred in the valleys and towns beyond. Loyalist bands and raiders still prowled the backroads, threatening the fragile calm. The war's shadow stretched long, and Elias knew the fight for freedom was far from over.

One evening, as twilight deepened, a rider arrived at the farm, dust coating his cloak and face. He brought word from the militia — more men were needed to defend the frontier, to hold the line against those who sought to undo their hard-won gains.

Elias's heart clenched. The call to arms was not done with him yet.

His father looked at him with steady eyes. "You have a duty, Elias. But remember, there's strength in building, too. Not all battles are fought with a sword or musket."

Elias nodded, torn between the warrior he had become and the boy who longed for peace.

That night, as the fire crackled low, Elias made his choice. He would stand ready — to fight if needed, but also to help heal the wounds of their land.

The road ahead was uncertain, but he was no longer the boy who left. He was a man forged by fire, bound by honor, and driven by hope.

And with each new dawn, he would build a future worthy of the sacrifices made.

Chapter 5

A rare calm fell over the valley, as if time itself had paused to take a breath. The low sun filtered softly through the canopy of oak and pine, dappling the forest floor with golden patches. The air smelled of fresh earth and blooming wildflowers, carrying the faint hum of bees and the distant call of songbirds. For the first time in months, the sound of musket fire and marching feet was replaced by the steady rhythm of daily life.

Elias stood on the small ridge overlooking the settlement, the cool breeze tugging at his worn jacket. Below, the farms were waking, smoke curling lazily from chimneys, horses nickered as they were saddled, and children's laughter echoed from the fields where they chased one another beneath the towering trees.

It was a scene so peaceful it almost felt unreal, like a painting too perfect to be true. But Elias knew better. He had learned the hard way that peace was often fragile — a delicate glass balanced on a knife's edge.

Yet today, the valley was calm. His breath deepened as he took it in, the weight of months of war slowly lifting from his shoulders.

Behind him, the forge's rhythmic clanging called him back to work. His father was already busy shaping horseshoes and repairing tools, the sparks flying like fireflies in the morning light.

Elias descended the ridge and joined him, the familiar heat of the forge warming his chilled skin. The metal sang beneath his hammer, steady and sure — a sharp contrast to the chaos that had marked their recent past.

"Feels like the world is holding its breath," his father said without looking up, sweat beading on his brow.

"Waiting for the next storm," Elias replied. "But maybe this calm can last a little longer."

His father nodded slowly. "We've earned a moment like this, boy. Don't forget that."

They worked side by side, the hours slipping away in shared silence. Outside, neighbors passed by with greetings and smiles, some carrying baskets of fresh eggs or jars of honey. The community was small but resilient, bound together by shared hardship and hope.

Elias's thoughts wandered to Samuel, to the brother he had lost. The ache in his chest was a dull constant, softened only by the knowledge that Samuel's sacrifice had not been in vain. Every life rebuilt, every fence mended, was a testament to his memory.

Later, Elias met with the other young men near the old oak at the village's edge. Caleb was already there, sharpening his knife, while others gathered with expressions ranging from hopeful to wary.

"The war's not over," Caleb said, breaking the silence. "We all know that."

Elias looked around at their faces — some scarred, some pale, all marked by what they'd endured.

"But while we can, we rebuild," Elias answered. "We hold this place. For our families, for the future."

The men nodded, understanding the unspoken truth — peace was a gift to be guarded, not taken for granted.

That afternoon, Elias wandered toward the creek that ran through the valley. The water bubbled over smooth stones, clear and cold. He sat on a moss-covered rock, watching the ripples catch the sunlight.

The simplicity of the moment was a balm, but his mind was restless. He knew the world beyond the trees was shifting. There were whispers of unrest — rumors of Loyalist bands gathering, of raids in neighboring settlements.

He pulled his coat tighter around him and scanned the distant hills. Beyond those rolling ridges lay unknown dangers, shadows creeping toward their fragile peace.

As the sun dipped low, Elias returned home to find his mother kneeling in the garden, hands deep in the soil. The scent of fresh herbs filled the air.

"Elias," she said softly, looking up. "You carry the weight of many battles in your eyes."

He smiled faintly. "It's the burden we all share."

She reached out, touching his cheek with a mother's quiet strength. "Remember to rest. Your spirit needs tending as much as your body."

Her words lingered long after dinner, as Elias sat by the hearth, the flickering flames casting dancing shadows on the walls. He pulled from his pocket the worn musket ball — a small, cold reminder of the past.

Tomorrow, he vowed, he would face whatever came next with steady heart. For now, he allowed himself this moment of fragile peace, holding tightly to the hope it brought.

The late afternoon sun cast long shadows across the valley as the steady clip-clop of hooves echoed along the dusty trail. The rhythmic sound cut through the usual chorus of birdsong and rustling leaves, drawing the attention of the men working near the trading post and the women hanging laundry or gathering herbs.

Elias was among those who paused to watch. His hand rested on the worn handle of his hunting knife, the muscles in his jaw tight with cautious curiosity. A solitary rider approached, a lone figure cloaked in dust and travel-worn clothes. His horse was lean and tired, its flanks streaked with sweat. Yet the man's posture was upright, his eyes sharp beneath a wide-brimmed hat.

The rider slowed as he neared the edge of the settlement, pulling the reins taut. A swirl of dust settled behind him as the horse came to a stop. The man dismounted with deliberate care, the leather of his boots scuffing against the dry earth. His face was streaked with grime and sweat, but his gaze was steady, locking onto Elias and the cluster of settlers now gathered.

"I'm Jonas Reed," the rider announced, voice hoarse from long days on the road. "I come with news — urgent news from the east."

A hush fell over the crowd. Elias stepped forward, stepping out from the shadows of the trees, feeling the weight of dozens of eyes on him.

"What news do you bring?" Elias asked, trying to keep his voice steady, though his heart beat faster.

Jonas took a deep breath, pushing back his hat to reveal a forehead creased with worry. "The Loyalists grow restless. Raids have been reported near the river settlements—farms burned, families scattered. They're moving closer to these parts, more brazen than before."

Murmurs spread like wildfire. Some faces paled, others hardened with resolve. Caleb, standing beside Elias, tightened his grip on the knife he held.

"How many? Are there more coming?" Caleb asked, eyes narrowing.

Jonas shook his head slowly. "I traveled ahead of the others to seek allies. For now, I'm alone. But if this settlement stands strong, others may follow."

Elias's mind raced. The valley had been spared much of the worst violence—until now. The hard-won peace felt as fragile as glass, and the fragile bubble seemed ready to burst.

The settlers exchanged anxious glances. The news was a bitter reminder that the war was far from over. Yet, in Jonas's presence, they found a renewed sense of purpose.

That evening, the settlement's small tavern filled with voices hushed but eager. Flames flickered in the hearth, casting long shadows on the rough-hewn walls as settlers leaned in to listen.

Jonas unfolded the stories like a map of both despair and hope.

He spoke of farms razed to the ground, of families driven from their homes by Loyalist bands, and of desperate patriots banding together to fight back. He described skirmishes near the river, fierce and unrelenting, where courage had kept hope alive.

"There are men willing to stand," Jonas said quietly, "but they need help. They need neighbors who will not turn away when the storm comes."

Elias's gaze wandered to the faces around him—young and old, each carrying scars of their own. Some had lost loved ones; others bore wounds hidden beneath their clothing. The stories stirred something deep within him — a flicker of determination that refused to be extinguished.

When the crowd began to thin, Elias noticed a young woman standing apart, clutching a folded letter close to her chest. Her dark eyes were steady, but the shadows beneath them spoke of sleepless nights and unspoken fears.

"Are you with him?" Elias asked gently, nodding toward Jonas.

"I am Miriam," she replied softly. "My family lived near the river settlements. We fled when the raids came. I came with Jonas, hoping to find safety here."

There was a strength in her voice, though it trembled just enough to reveal the depth of her sorrow.

Elias stepped closer, offering a small smile. "You're safe now. We'll do everything we can."

She returned the smile, a fragile but hopeful expression.

Over the coming days, Miriam became a part of the community — a steady presence in the settling dust. She helped tend to the wounded and cared for children who had lost their mothers. Her stories painted vivid pictures of the lands beyond the hills, of homes shattered and lives uprooted.

At the same time, the arrival of strangers awakened old fears in some of the settlers. Whispers floated in the marketplace—suspicions of spies or hidden enemies among them. The wounds of past betrayals were slow to heal.

One afternoon, Elias found Miriam sitting alone by the creek, the water running clear and cold over smooth stones.

He sat beside her, watching the sunlight play on the ripples.

"Do you think we'll ever be free from this?" she asked, voice barely above a whisper.

Elias looked out toward the distant hills. "I want to believe so. But freedom comes at a price. We fight, we lose, we keep going."

Miriam nodded, her eyes reflecting the fading light. "I want to build a future where my children don't have to hide in the woods."

"We will," Elias promised. "Together."

Their hands found each other's, a quiet promise in a world full of uncertainty.

Yet, beneath the fragile hope, Elias felt the weight of the coming storm. The valley was no longer isolated from the tides of war. The settlers had to prepare — not just for survival, but for the fight to protect what they loved most.

The days grew shorter, the sun dipping earlier behind the ridge of hills that cradled the valley. Crisp air swept down from the mountain tops, carrying the scent of pine and damp earth mixed with the smoke from wood fires. The approach of autumn was unmistakable, but the season's usual quiet was absent this year. Instead, the valley hummed with an uneasy tension, as if the land itself sensed the turmoil gathering beyond its borders.

Elias stood atop a knoll that overlooked the settlement, hands resting on the worn wooden railing of the lookout platform Caleb had built. The view was familiar — cabins nestled among the trees, the small trading post's weathered roof catching the last glimmers of daylight, smoke rising in lazy spirals from chimneys. Yet, in the warm golden light, everything seemed fragile, suspended on a knife's edge.

Below, figures moved with purpose. Men sharpened blades and stacked firewood; women tended to gardens, their eyes wary but steady. Children played cautiously near the creek, their laughter fleeting and nervous.

Elias's gaze settled on Miriam, crouched beside the herb garden behind the tavern. Her fingers worked deftly through the soil, pulling weeds and coaxing the last blooms from late-season plants. There was a softness in the curve of her shoulders, a quiet strength in the set of her jaw. To Elias, she was a beacon amid the encroaching darkness — a reminder that life could still flourish even when shadows pressed close.

He felt the familiar ache settle in his chest — the ache of responsibility, of hope intertwined with fear.

Inside the tavern, the air was thick with the scent of burning wood and earth. The low murmur of voices rose and fell like the tide. By the hearth, Caleb sat with a group of men, the steel edge of his knife flashing as he methodically sharpened the blade. His brow was drawn tight, eyes sharp beneath the heavy lines etched by years of hardship.

"We can't wait for the enemy to come knocking on our doors," one man argued, a burly fellow with a scar running from cheek to chin. "We need scouts out in the woods. Patrols every dawn and dusk. Every man ready to draw his weapon if trouble shows."

Caleb nodded slowly, his gaze flickering toward Elias as the young leader entered the room. "He's right. This valley has been a refuge, but we can't let our guard down. We need to be prepared — ready to fight or flee if necessary."

The men exchanged grim looks, the weight of the coming conflict settling on their shoulders.

Elias drew a deep breath, feeling the mantle of leadership pressing heavier with every passing day. "It's not just about weapons or patrols," he said, voice firm but calm. "We need to build trust — between the old settlers and the newcomers. Between families who've lived here for years and those who've only just arrived."

Jonas Reed, seated near the fire, nodded in agreement. His face was gaunt, his eyes sharp beneath heavy brows. "Suspicion is natural," he said quietly. "But if we fracture ourselves now, the enemy wins without lifting a finger."

Elias scanned the room, catching glimpses of doubt in some faces, hope in others. The arrival of refugees like Miriam and her family had not been universally welcomed. Whispers of spies and hidden enemies had crept into the marketplace, souring the fragile peace.

That evening, Elias found himself walking the perimeter of the settlement alongside Caleb and Jonas. The fading light painted the trees in deep shadow, the air thick with the scent of pine needles and moss.

"We'll need more than just guards," Caleb said, his voice low. "We'll need a system — signals, safe houses, a way to warn everyone if danger approaches."

Jonas nodded thoughtfully. "And we'll need to learn the terrain better. The Loyalists know these woods well. We need to match their knowledge."

Elias looked out into the gathering darkness. The valley was beautiful — peaceful on the surface — but beneath, currents of unease twisted like hidden roots.

"We start at dawn," Elias said. "Scouts will head into the woods. We'll learn what's out there before they find us."

The night deepened, stars sparking cold and distant overhead. As Elias returned to the tavern, he found Miriam sitting by the fire, her hands wrapped around a tin cup. The flickering flames cast warm light on her pale face, highlighting the shadows beneath her eyes.

"You've been working hard," Elias said softly, sitting beside her.

She smiled faintly. "The garden helps keep my mind busy. And it's good to be useful."

Her gaze drifted to the door, as if expecting someone or something.

"Do you ever think about the future?" Elias asked, wanting to pierce the veil of uncertainty.

She nodded slowly. "Every day. I imagine a life beyond fear — children playing without looking over their shoulders, neighbors helping neighbors instead of watching for spies."

Her voice was steady, but Elias sensed the heavy weight behind the words — the dreams shadowed by loss.

"We'll get there," Elias promised. "We have to."

Their conversation was interrupted by a sudden knock on the tavern door. Elias rose, moving to open it cautiously. A young boy, no older than ten, stood on the threshold, his face pale and eyes wide.

"Sir," the boy whispered urgently, "there's someone watching from the trees near the north ridge. He won't come down, but he's been there all evening."

Elias's heart quickened. "Stay here. Don't make a sound."

He stepped outside into the cool night air, his breath forming small clouds in the dark. He scanned the tree line, eyes straining against the shadows.

There — a figure crouched low, barely visible against the blackened trunks. The man moved silently, watching the settlement with cold, calculating eyes.

Elias's grip tightened on his knife. The enemy was closer than they'd realized.

Returning to the tavern, Elias gathered the others. "We have a watcher," he announced grimly. "The Loyalists are scouting us. We must be ready — at all times."

The room fell silent, the weight of the threat sinking deep.

Miriam stepped forward, her voice steady despite the fear flickering in her eyes. "We've come this far together. We won't let them break us now."

Her words stirred a fire in the hearts of the settlers. They would fight. They would survive. Because the valley was more than just land — it was home.

But as the night deepened, Elias knew the road ahead would be perilous. The fragile peace had shattered, and the valley would never be the same.

The night after the watcher was spotted, the valley fell under a suffocating blanket of silence, as if the earth itself was holding its breath. Shadows stretched long and cold, twisting with the flickering light of campfires and lanterns. Sleep became a stranger to the settlement, chased off by the slightest sound: the snap of a twig, the rustle of a leaf, the whispered footfalls of patrols moving through the darkness.

Elias lay on his cot in the small room behind the tavern, eyes wide open, staring at the rough-hewn ceiling. The weight of the past weeks pressed heavily on his chest, each memory folding into the next. The faces of those who had fled violence, the hopeful smiles that masked deep scars, the steady hands ready to fight — all demanded his attention. The responsibility that had fallen on him wasn't just about strategy or survival; it was about the future of everyone he cared for.

He sat up, running a hand through tangled hair, his mind racing with what-ifs. *If we fail, what becomes of Miriam? Of the children? Of the valley itself?* The thought stung sharper than any blade.

Outside, the wind whispered through the trees, carrying the scent of pine and wet earth. A lone owl hooted, breaking the oppressive quiet. Elias rose and stepped onto the porch, the cool night air biting his skin. He squinted into the blackness of the woods that bordered the settlement, where shadows melded and shifted like living things.

The next morning brought no relief. A pale, cold sun rose over the hills, casting a weak light on a land poised on the edge of ruin. Men gathered at the tavern before dawn, voices low but tense. Caleb's face was set hard, eyes narrowed with concern as he outlined the morning's patrol.

"We send out three groups," Caleb said, pointing to rough sketches of the surrounding forest marked on a battered piece of parchment. "One to the north ridge where the watcher was seen, another to the east along the creek, and a third to scout the old logging trail. We need to know what's out there before they find us."

Jonas adjusted his worn hat and stepped forward, his voice calm but edged with urgency. "The Loyalists know these woods like the back of their hand. We'll need every advantage — tracking, camouflage, silence."

Elias felt the weight of their gazes on him. Though young, he was the one who must lead. His voice was steady as he added, "We'll rotate the patrols daily. Every able-bodied person, trained and ready. And we need lookouts posted at night — no exceptions."

The group murmured assent. The mood was grim, but a flicker of determination glimmered beneath the surface.

As the patrols disappeared into the thick woods, Elias lingered near the tavern's entrance, watching the treeline as if willing the shadows to reveal their secrets. Miriam appeared beside him, her breath visible in the chill morning air.

"They're brave," she said quietly. "But this isn't just a fight over land. It's a battle for hope."

Elias looked at her — the firelight catching in her dark eyes — and nodded. "If we lose that, everything else falls apart."

Days stretched into weeks, each one heavier than the last. The settlers worked tirelessly, reinforcing fences with sharpened stakes, digging trenches, and setting traps along the less visible paths. Even the children learned to move silently, disappearing into the woods for hours at a time to watch and listen.

Inside the tavern, the heart of the valley's community, lessons were under-way. Caleb taught musket loading and basic swordplay. Elias demonstrated tracking signs in the underbrush, while Jonas shared stories of the land, teaching the settlers to read the whispering woods and the subtle shifts in the weather.

At times, the weight of it all fractured their fragile unity. Some whispered that Elias was too young, too inexperienced to lead them through such darkness. Others eyed the newcomers with suspicion, fearful that spies lurked among them. Rumors twisted through the settlement like poison — a broken trust that threatened to unravel their carefully woven community.

One evening, as cold rain hammered against the tavern windows and lightning tore the sky, Elias called a meeting. The room was packed with faces marked by exhaustion and fear. The firelight danced over the walls, casting giant shadows that flickered with every crack of thunder.

"I know many of you have doubts," Elias began, his voice echoing in the small space. "I don't pretend to have all the answers. But I stand here because I believe in us — in every person willing to fight for this valley and each other."

He scanned the room, meeting eyes that shone with hope and others clouded with mistrust. "This war is not just a battle of muskets and blades. It's a battle for trust, for unity. If we fracture now, we give our enemies the victory before a shot is fired."

The silence that followed was thick but sincere. Slowly, hands began to clap — hesitant at first, then growing stronger. Miriam stepped forward, her voice steady and clear above the din.

"We've all lost much. Our homes, our families, our peace. But we still have each other. We'll build this valley into a home worth fighting for."

Outside, the wind howled and rain hammered the earth, but inside, hope flickered like a stubborn flame.

Yet, even as the settlers rallied, the natural world reminded them that danger was never far. Wolves prowled the forests, their eerie howls echoing through the night. The wildness around them was a constant reminder that the land they fought to protect was as unpredictable as the human heart.

One afternoon, Elias and Miriam walked through the village square, now fortified with stakes and trenches. Children played warily near the creek, their laughter tinged with nervous energy. Farmers worked their fields with grim determination, glancing often toward the woods.

Elias stopped at the trading post, where Jonas was busy sharpening knives. The old man looked up and nodded, a weathered smile breaking through his stoic expression.

"You're doing good, Elias," Jonas said. "Leadership isn't just about orders. It's about knowing the people — their fears, their strengths."

Elias nodded thoughtfully. "I just hope it's enough."

Suddenly, a scout burst through the square, panting and wide-eyed. "Enemy patrol spotted near the south ridge! They're moving fast, and there's more of them than we thought."

A hush fell over the crowd, the tension snapping taut like a drawn bowstring.

"Sound the alarm," Elias ordered, his voice ringing with urgency. "To your posts! Prepare to defend the valley."

The settlers moved with practiced speed, men grabbing weapons, women ushering children to safety, older boys taking up positions at the lookouts.

Elias felt his heart pounding as he ran to the tavern, grabbing a musket and checking its load. Miriam appeared at his side, eyes fierce.

"This is it," she said. "We stand together."

As the first distant sounds of hoofbeats and voices reached their ears, Elias gripped his weapon tighter. The valley, once a place of quiet refuge, had become a battleground. And he, a young leader forged by necessity, was ready to meet the storm head-on.

The morning light seeped slowly over the edge of the mountains, but it brought no peace.

Elias McCrae stood on the western ridge, the musket in his hands slick with dew. Beneath his boots, the frost-laced grass crackled softly with every shift of his weight. He could smell woodsmoke from the settler camp behind him, mingling with the sharper tang of oiled metal and powder. The valley below, shadowed and still, waited like a held breath.

Caleb crouched nearby, peering through a spyglass toward the narrow pass.

"They'll come from the hollow," Caleb said, his voice low and certain. "It's the only opening wide enough to march through with any force."

Elias glanced sidelong at him. "They're Loyalists?"

"Some. Militia mostly, likely with British backing. Could be Ferguson's men—or sympathizers from further east." Caleb lowered the glass. "No time to figure out who. Only how to stop them."

Behind them, the settlers were awake and grimly preparing. Old men loaded muskets with shaking hands. Teenagers—barely older than Elias—fumbled with powder horns, their faces pale. Mothers bound their sons' wrists with strips of linen, talismans for survival. One woman sharpened a kitchen knife with the same care she once used slicing apples for pie.

Miriam passed through them like a quiet fire, giving out water, offering reassurances, binding splinters of fear with threads of resolve.

"Elias," she said gently, coming to stand beside him. "Are you ready?"

He hesitated. Was he? He was just a boy from a forge. A blacksmith's son who'd once been more afraid of singeing his sleeves than firing a gun.

But there was no room for hesitation now.

"I have to be," he answered. "We all do."

She nodded and squeezed his shoulder. "Watch yourself."

Then, a sound—barely more than the breeze at first. A rustle. Then the unmistakable *crack* of a branch underfoot. Caleb's hand went to his musket.

"There," he whispered, pointing toward the tree line. "Movement."

They crouched low. In the distance, shadows flickered between the trunks—figures, dressed in brown and gray, flitting fast and low like wolves on the prowl.

"Don't shoot yet," Caleb muttered. "Wait until they commit."

The valley tensed. The settlers, hidden in the ridges and among the trees, held their breath. Elias's pulse thudded in his ears.

A sharp whistle sliced through the air—then the woods exploded.

Men in coats surged from the forest like a dam broken, muskets raised. Loyalist flags waved briefly before vanishing behind smoke and gunfire.

"Fire!" Caleb bellowed.

Elias pulled the trigger, and his musket roared. The recoil shoved into his shoulder like a punch. The air filled with smoke, then screams.

From behind the ridgeline, settlers sprang to their feet and unleashed hell. Arrows flew from Cherokee bows. Muskets barked. The enemy faltered under the sudden, furious defense.

But they didn't break.

Elias reloaded on instinct, pouring powder with shaking fingers, ramming the ball home. A Loyalist soldier rushed the embankment—Elias aimed and fired, the man crumpling mid-charge.

Beside him, Caleb took a hit to the arm but kept firing, gritting his teeth.

"We can't let them flank the pass!" he shouted. "Hold them here!"

A trio of Loyalists scrambled up a side trail—Elias shouted a warning. Jonas, crouched nearby with two teenage boys, pivoted and cut them down with clean, practiced shots.

"Stay in pairs!" Jonas barked. "Don't get isolated!"

Across the field, the valley became a battlefield in truth. The smoke thickened until faces disappeared in it. Fires ignited where bullets struck dry brush. A cabin roof caught, its thatch burning like tinder.

Women dragged the wounded back behind wagons turned into barricades. Miriam was everywhere—kneeling beside a boy whose leg was bleeding badly, shouting for bandages, pressing rags into wounds with furious tenderness.

"Stay with me," she said, over and over. "You're going to stay with me."

Elias caught sight of her just before he ducked behind a felled tree. He fired blind into the smoke and hoped it found a target.

Suddenly, the ground in front of him exploded—he fell backward, ears ringing, dirt in his mouth.

"Elias!" someone shouted.

Caleb grabbed his jacket and pulled him down into a ditch.

"You alright?"

"I—I think so," Elias panted. His cheek burned, scraped from the fall, but he was whole. For now.

"Then get up. We're not finished."

They climbed out together and pushed back toward the center of the ridge. Loyalists were gaining ground there, pressing hard toward the church near the heart of the valley. Elias spotted three of them setting fire to a wagon.

He aimed, but one saw him first—he ducked just as the bullet whistled past. Caleb took the shot instead, clean through the chest. The Loyalist dropped.

"Elias, move!" Miriam's voice cried out.

He looked back—one of the settlers was lying on the path behind him, bleeding from a gut wound. Without thinking, Elias dragged the man back to cover, grunting from the effort. He barely recognized the face—it was a farmer from three valleys over—but he pressed his hand over the wound.

"Stay with me. You're alright. We've got you," he said.

Miriam was there in a moment. "Let me—Elias, go. Go!"

Elias stood, shaking, and turned back to the line.

By late afternoon, the fighting slowed. The Loyalists were pulling back, dragging their wounded through the woods. A few settlers gave chase, but Caleb called them back.

"We're not hunters today," he said. "We're defenders. Let them run."

The smoke settled slowly. Elias leaned on his musket and looked out over what had once been a peaceful clearing. Now it was trampled earth, blood-streaked and littered with broken tools and spent cartridges.

Bodies lay still in the golden grass. Some settlers. Some enemies. All sons of the same soil.

He found Miriam sitting near the well, her hands covered in dried blood. Her dress was torn. Her face was smeared with soot.

"You saved him," she said, her voice hoarse. "The man you pulled from the trail. He's alive."

Elias sat beside her, exhaustion pressing into his bones. "We held the valley."

She nodded, looking out over the smoke-streaked fields. "For now."

"I thought…" He hesitated. "I thought when the time came, I'd be ready. That all my thinking, all my training, would make it easier."

Miriam met his eyes. "It never gets easier. But it matters."

Behind them, the camp stirred with the quiet rituals of aftermath—bodies being covered, fires being doused, food being shared among the living. Caleb was giving orders again, arm bandaged tight. Jonas walked the line, checking every face for the ones he feared he wouldn't find.

Elias saw a boy—maybe twelve—staring at his hands, red with someone else's blood. An older woman knelt beside him, pressing his fingers around a cup of water.

"We'll dig in deeper," Elias said aloud. "Fortify the trail. They'll come again."

"They will," Miriam replied. "But next time… we'll be stronger."

He looked out once more at the valley. His valley. The place his father had called home. The place where Samuel's bones rested beneath the tree line. A land bought in sweat and defended now in blood.

"We'll hold it," Elias said. "However many times it takes."

As night fell, the stars appeared one by one, like watchful eyes above them. Fires glowed faint and low. Somewhere, someone began to hum—a low, mournful tune that spread slowly among the survivors, not a song of victory, but of remembrance.

The first clash was over.

But Elias knew the war had only just begun.

Chapter 6

Morning broke quiet, yet the stillness felt uneasy. A thick fog hung low over the ridge, clinging to the twisted trees like ghosts reluctant to leave. The smoke from last night's campfires curled faintly into the gray light, trailing upward into nothingness. Elias stood near the edge of the timberline, shovel in hand, boots caked with blood-muddied earth.

They had dug the first grave just after dawn.

There was no ceremony. No pastor. No folded hands in reverence. Only the dull sound of dirt hitting wood, and the groans of men trying not to cry. Elias's arms ached from the digging, his blisters torn and raw. He tried not to look at the faces they were lowering into the earth, but some he recognized. That made it worse. Names he didn't know yesterday now pressed into him like iron.

An older man from Virginia named Clay had died clutching a letter from a daughter he never got to answer. A boy from the Nolichucky, younger than Elias, had bled out in silence behind a boulder, a hole in his chest the size of a musket ball. There were nine men altogether. One more died after sunrise, bringing the total to ten.

Ten lives gone. Ten families that would never see their sons, brothers, or husbands again.

Jonas worked beside Elias, quieter than usual. His face was drawn and pale, eyes sunken from the strain of leadership. Elias had watched him step over the bodies at first light, whispering their names to himself before motioning for the digging to begin. He carried their deaths like stones in his chest.

"You sleep at all?" Jonas asked after a long silence.

Elias shook his head. "Didn't feel right. Not with all that…" He gestured vaguely toward the row of covered bodies.

Jonas nodded and dug another spade of dirt. "No. It didn't."

Somewhere in the distance, an ax rang against wood—someone chopping pine to build more stretchers. Miriam's voice echoed briefly across the clearing, ordering her younger brother to fetch water. The camp stirred like a wounded beast, groaning to life beneath its grief.

Elias wiped the back of his hand across his face, smearing dirt across his cheek. "They ambushed us, Jonas. We weren't ready."

"No," Jonas agreed grimly. "But we will be."

The grave was nearly full now. Elias stepped back, handing Jonas the shovel. His arms trembled from fatigue, but he didn't want to show it. He glanced around the camp—faces gaunt, eyes hollow. Even the animals sensed the tension. The horses didn't nicker or paw the earth like usual. They stood still, quiet, heads down.

Near the treeline, Caleb Sharp sat with his back against a stump, his rifle across his lap. He looked younger somehow, like the bloodshed had peeled back a layer of arrogance Elias hadn't even noticed was there. Caleb caught Elias's gaze and gave a small nod. Elias returned it, unsure what it meant— approval, apology, or just shared survival.

Suddenly, the woods stirred. Everyone tensed.

A scout emerged from the brush, his coat torn, face streaked with sweat and dirt. He moved quickly, whispering to one of the sentries before making his way toward Jonas.

"They're moving," the scout said without preamble. "Loyalists. Maybe sixty, seventy men. Heading northeast. Might be regrouping."

Jonas narrowed his eyes. "How far?"

"Two ridges over. Not more than ten miles."

Caleb stood and slung his rifle over his shoulder. "We should hit them now, before they settle."

"We don't even know their strength yet," Jonas replied, measured. "Rushing in half-blind didn't go so well last time."

The scout glanced over his shoulder as if the trees might spit out soldiers at any moment. "We've got hours at best."

Jonas looked to Elias, then back toward the camp. "We'll regroup. Decide by midday."

The scout nodded and vanished back into the trees.

Elias walked toward the creek to wash his hands. The cold water stung as it touched his cracked skin. His reflection stared back at him—dirty, hollow-eyed, and older than he remembered. He barely recognized himself anymore.

The first time he'd held a rifle, it had felt like a burden. Now it felt like an extension of him, part of his body. And that scared him.

He heard footsteps behind him.

"Elias," Miriam said, crouching beside him. Her sleeves were rolled to her elbows, stained with dried blood. She smelled of pine resin and smoke. "There's something in your hair," she murmured, reaching out.

Elias flinched slightly, but she only picked a twig from the back of his head.

"You're filthy," she added with a faint smile.

"So are you," he replied.

She chuckled, but the sound was tired. "You holding up?"

He didn't answer right away. The water ran cold over his fingers, rushing over the stones like nothing had happened. "We buried ten men this morning," he finally said.

"I know."

"They didn't cry. Not even the ones who lost brothers."

"They'll cry later. Or maybe they won't."

Elias nodded, then looked at her, really looked. Her face was smudged and her eyes bloodshot, but her expression held something steady. Strong. He wanted to ask how she stayed that way, but the words wouldn't come.

"You think it'll get worse?" he asked instead.

Miriam didn't lie. "Yes."

The answer hit harder than he expected. She stood and offered her hand. He took it, letting her pull him up. "Then we better be ready," he said.

The midday sun began to burn away the fog. Shadows shortened and the air warmed, but the mood stayed cold. Jonas gathered the men beneath a cluster of cedar trees, spreading out maps and marking potential routes in the dirt with a stick. Elias stayed near the edge of the group, listening.

"We need eyes ahead," Jonas said. "Before we move."

"I'll go," Elias said quickly, before he could think twice.

Several heads turned. Jonas studied him. "You sure?"

Elias squared his shoulders. "Yes, sir."

Jonas didn't smile, but his eyes softened. "Then we'll send you with two others. Caleb and Joseph. Head out before dusk. Track them. Watch, don't engage. Return before sunrise."

Elias nodded. "Yes, sir."

As the meeting broke, Caleb approached and clapped Elias on the shoulder. "Guess you and I are stuck together again."

Elias didn't reply. He was already watching the horizon, already thinking about what lay ahead—about what kind of man he was becoming, and whether he'd still recognize himself when this was over.

Far off, across the ridge, a hawk circled silently in the pale sky.

They left the camp just before dusk.

The light filtering through the canopy had turned a burnt gold, slanting across their faces and casting long shadows through the brush. Elias moved near the front, just behind Joseph, who carried a long rifle and walked with the certainty of a man who had tracked foxes in this wilderness long before he'd tracked men. Caleb brought up the rear, quieter than usual, though his eyes darted to every snapping twig and shifting branch.

The woods were thick with silence. Not peace—there was nothing peaceful about this part of the world now—but a tense, almost waiting kind of stillness. The kind of silence that comes before a storm, or after a death.

"We'll cut northeast across the gulch," Joseph murmured, his voice barely louder than the wind. "There's a split ridge with high ground near a rock face. If they're camped nearby, we'll see them from there."

Elias nodded. He moved more carefully now, placing each foot with thought, trying to match the pace of the older men. The overmountain march had toughened his legs and stripped away the boyish clumsiness he carried back in Watauga. He felt leaner now. Stronger. Sharper. But he didn't yet know if he was braver.

They crossed a narrow stream and wound their way up a forested rise where old birches bent in crooked shapes like hunched ghosts. Elias stopped for a breath and touched the bark of one—its skin thin and peeling. He thought of the grave they dug for Clay. Thought of Clay's daughter, of the letter he never got to answer.

"Keep moving," Caleb hissed behind him.

By twilight, they reached the ridge.

Joseph held up a fist, signaling for them to crouch. All three dropped to a low crawl, slipping through brush until they found cover behind a line of boulders that overlooked a bowl-shaped clearing below. The air smelled of ash.

"There," Joseph whispered.

Smoke rose faintly from beyond the trees on the far end of the basin. Camp-fires. Figures moved in the fading light, small and blurry but unmistakably human.

"Loyalists?" Elias asked.

"No one else would be camped out here this deep," Caleb muttered.

Joseph adjusted his hat and narrowed his eyes. "Can't be sure how many. Could be fifty, maybe more. Hard to tell."

They watched in silence for several minutes. Elias noticed the lack of flags, the sloppy spacing between tents. These weren't soldiers in tight formation— these were backwoods fighters, just like them. But they had something dangerous about them. A kind of confidence that came from blood already spilled.

"See that?" Caleb pointed to a cluster of three riders tethering their horses beneath a bluff. "They're settling in. Probably think we're still licking our wounds."

"We are," Joseph muttered. "But we'll bleed 'em back."

The sky faded from purple to deep blue. An owl called once from the distant trees. Joseph leaned close.

"We'll move along the western rim," he said. "Circle around and take a closer look from the ridge above their camp. We leave no sign. No scent. Not a single snapped twig."

They moved like shadows through the darkness.

Elias found that his breathing matched the rhythm of his steps—shallow, quiet, in through the nose. He remembered his brother Samuel's advice during hunting seasons: "The forest listens. Every mistake you make, it echoes." Elias had laughed back then. He wasn't laughing now.

The stars blinked through the treetops. Somewhere an animal moved through the brush, and all three scouts froze. It passed, silent but close. Elias felt sweat bead down his spine. When they moved again, he was even more careful.

They reached a ledge overlooking the enemy camp just after full night fell. From here, they had a better view: tents arranged in a crescent, a ring of sentries moving lazily at the edge. Fires burned low. Laughter drifted faintly upward—coarse, unbothered laughter. The kind of laughter men used when they thought they were safe.

"Too many," Joseph whispered. "We won't get a headcount tonight, not with them moving like that."

"They're expecting someone," Caleb murmured. "Look there." He pointed to the bluff. "That's not a normal lookout. That's an ambush post."

Elias studied the bluff. Two men sat on a perch above the ridge, rifles in hand, their eyes sweeping the woods even in darkness.

"Could be a trap," Elias said.

"Could be they're just careful," Joseph replied. "Hard to know until we see what they do come morning."

"Do we wait it out?" Caleb asked.

Joseph didn't answer right away. Finally, he said, "We give it another hour. Then we move out. If they shift position, we follow."

The three hunkered behind the ridge, barely breathing. Time passed in long stretches, measured only by firelight flickers and the soft rustling of wind in leaves.

Elias's legs cramped. He shifted slightly, careful not to disturb the moss beneath him.

"You ever wonder what you'd be doing if none of this happened?" he whispered to Caleb.

Caleb didn't respond at first. "Every day."

Elias glanced at him in the moonlight. "What would it be?"

Caleb's eyes were fixed on the camp. "Trapping in the highlands, probably. Maybe running a post near French Broad. You?"

"I'd still be pounding iron. Probably apprenticed now. Maybe married." Elias smiled faintly. "Or at least pretending I'm not afraid to ask Miriam's father."

Caleb snorted quietly. "You and half the valley."

"Does it ever get easier?" Elias asked. "The… fear? The killing?"

Caleb shifted, face unreadable. "No. You just get better at hiding it."

Joseph grunted softly from beside them. "That's enough talking."

The wind shifted, blowing smoke from the Loyalist fires toward them. Elias caught the faint smell of roasted meat—boar or deer, it was hard to tell. His stomach tightened, not from hunger but unease. These men weren't starving. They were supplied, confident, rested. They weren't preparing to flee. They were waiting for something.

Suddenly, a loud whistle sounded from below—sharp and quick. Movement stirred instantly. The camp bristled with life. Men scrambled toward the fire pits, stamping them out. Torches flared. Horses neighed in protest.

"They're spooked," Joseph whispered.

"What triggered them?" Caleb asked.

Elias leaned forward. Then he saw it.

Two figures stumbled out of the trees on the far side of the camp, hands tied, blindfolded. Loyalist guards dragged them forward. Prisoners.

"They caught scouts," Elias said.

"Not ours," Joseph replied. "I don't recognize them."

But the thought sent a chill through Elias. Whoever those men were, they'd walked into something they didn't see coming.

The prisoners were forced to their knees. One shouted something—inaudible from their distance, but the defiance in his voice was clear. A guard struck him with the butt of a musket. The man fell, then rose slowly, blood streaking his chin.

Elias felt sick. His knuckles whitened around the stock of his rifle.

"Can't do anything for them now," Joseph said quietly. "We go back. Tell Jonas."

"What if they're Overmountain?" Elias whispered.

Caleb stared down. "Then they'll die like we might."

Joseph clapped them both on the shoulder. "Let's move. Carefully."

They retraced their steps, slipping back into the brush, wrapping shadows around them like cloaks. When they paused to rest near the gulch, Elias finally let out a breath he didn't know he'd been holding.

"I hate leaving them," he said.

Joseph nodded. "So do I. But sometimes the smartest thing is the hardest."

Elias looked up at the stars. Cold and silent. Watching everything.

"We'll come back for them," he said quietly. "One way or another."

Caleb gave him a look—hard, but not unkind. "That sounded like a vow."

Elias met his gaze. "Maybe it was."

They slipped back into the woods, three shadows among countless trees, carrying blood and oath in equal measure.

They returned to camp in the early hours before dawn. The sky was a slate of dark gray, the air heavy with moisture as if the forest itself had been holding its breath all night. Elias moved swiftly, his legs aching, sweat dried stiff on his brow. Behind him, Caleb and Joseph were grim and silent, the urgency of their discovery still fresh in every footstep.

A few sentries stirred from their lean-tos as the three men approached, eyes wary but recognizing them quickly enough to wave them through.

Inside the camp, the fires were embers and the men were bundles of cloaks and rifles, hunched shapes lost in exhaustion. Elias pushed past sleeping bodies until they reached the central ridge where Jonas sat upright on a log beside the fire pit, sharpening a knife in a rhythm that spoke of nerves.

He looked up as they approached. "Well?"

Joseph didn't waste time. "They're dug in on the other side of the gulch. Fifty men at least. Loyalists. Maybe more."

Jonas stopped sharpening. His eyes narrowed. "Armed?"

"Better than us in some ways," Caleb said. "Saw horses, saw rifles, and they've got meat and fire. Supplies are strong."

"And discipline?" Jonas asked.

Elias shook his head. "No formation. No colors. Just men in patches of gray and brown, carrying long guns and drinking like they're not afraid."

"They're waiting for something," Joseph added. "Could be an ambush. Might be a rendezvous."

Jonas stood slowly. "Did you see a standard? Flags?"

"None," said Caleb.

"But they've got prisoners," Elias added. "Two men dragged out of the trees. Hands bound, blindfolded. Might be settlers, or militia scouts."

The fire crackled. Jonas turned away, brow furrowed.

"That means they're confident enough to keep men alive," Caleb said. "They're not moving yet. Just holding."

"They're either waiting for Ferguson," Jonas murmured, "or baiting us into something."

A voice stirred behind them. "Sounds like a trap to me."

It was Colonel Shelby, still rubbing sleep from his face as he approached. His rifle leaned against one shoulder, his beard unkempt and flecked with ash. Isaac Shelby rarely rose before dawn unless trouble roused him—and the fire in his eyes now suggested he sensed a storm building.

"Fifty men or more is no small force," he said. "We can't just rush 'em."

Joseph nodded. "No, sir."

Colonel Campbell soon joined them, his breath visible in the cold morning air. "What else?"

Elias stepped forward. "They had a bluff—higher ground—with sentries posted above the camp. A good view in all directions. They'll see us coming before we're halfway there."

Campbell's jaw tightened. "Then we don't go straight at them."

The leadership gathered quickly after that—McDowell, Sevier, a few senior captains. The fire was stoked again, not for warmth but clarity, as if flames might burn away confusion. Elias stood just behind Jonas, watching the commanders form a circle and mark rough outlines in the dirt.

"What are you standing there for?" Shelby asked him suddenly. "You scouted. You've seen it. Speak."

Elias blinked. "Sir?"

"You saw with your own eyes," Shelby said. "So tell us what matters."

Elias looked at the rough map sketched in dirt—ridges and streams, a gulch, fire pits, a crescent of tents.

"The camp looks relaxed, but they're too well-positioned for that to be chance," he said. "Sentries on the ridge. Tents spread wide, not clustered. They're prepared for fire from any direction. But they're not forming ranks. Either they're undisciplined, or they're buying time."

"Good," Shelby nodded. "And what would you do, if you were them?"

Elias hesitated. "I'd delay us. Keep us guessing. Wait for a bigger force to join."

Shelby looked at Campbell. "That boy's sharper than he looks."

Elias flushed, but Jonas clapped him on the shoulder.

"I say we strike at dusk," Sevier said. "Under cover of woods. Break them before they expect it."

"We don't have the numbers," Campbell countered. "Fifty entrenched men in trees is worth a hundred charging up a slope."

"We do have surprise," Joseph added. "They didn't see us."

"We'll only have it once," Caleb warned.

Campbell leaned on his musket. "Then maybe we make them come to us."

"What do you mean?" McDowell asked.

"We bait them back," Campbell said. "Make it seem like we're retreating into the gulch. Lead a detachment away from camp and cut it down. Thin the herd."

"Too risky," Sevier said. "We might split too far."

"But we can't stay here forever," Jonas said. "Food's already running thin."

That truth lingered heavier than any order. The camp was low on flour. Salted pork was dwindling. Powder had to be rationed.

"If we don't move," Elias said quietly, "they'll come for us. When they're stronger. Better supplied."

Shelby looked at him again, and something in his expression shifted. Not quite fatherly, but something like recognition. "You've got the eyes of someone who's seen it coming."

Elias lowered his gaze. "I've seen too much, sir."

Jonas finally stepped in. "Give us one day. We move at night. Take the ridge they're watching from, flank them at dawn. A single volley from above will scatter a poorly trained camp."

Campbell considered. "Can your boys climb that bluff?"

"Elias can," Jonas said. "And so can I."

Elias blinked. "Wait—me?"

"You started this," Jonas said. "Might as well finish it."

That evening, preparations began.

The camp shifted from slumber to quiet urgency. Rifles were cleaned. Boots patched. Powder horns filled and checked again. Jonas walked Elias through the bluff terrain, pointing out where the pine knots could be used as holds and where a slip could mean a snapped leg or worse.

Caleb approached near sunset with an oilskin bundle. "You're climbing tonight. Figured you could use this."

He handed Elias a short belt knife—sleek, balanced.

"Thanks," Elias said.

"Don't get cocky," Caleb replied. "You're no ghost yet."

Later, just as the sun vanished behind the far ridge, Elias sat alone near the edge of camp. The firelight was far behind him. The stars were beginning to show.

He thought of his mother. Of her face at the door. Of Samuel. Of Miriam. He pulled out the scrap of paper he kept from home—his brother's last note—and read it again. The words blurred in the dark, but he didn't need to see them anymore. They were burned into him.

Stay strong. Do right. Come back with your soul.

Jonas found him just after moonrise. "Time."

The ridge climb was cruel.

They left with two others—Joseph and a young rifleman named Abram. The four moved like whispers through the trees, every branch avoided, every patch of pine needles stepped over carefully. The bluff loomed ahead, black and jagged against the stars.

Elias stared up at it and swallowed hard.

"You climb first," Jonas said. "You make it up quiet, you signal. If you fall, we wait for the scream. If there's no scream, we wait for silence."

Elias nodded. His hands trembled for a moment—then stilled.

The rock was colder than he expected. Moss clung to its face in patches, slick with dew. Elias moved slowly, carefully. His foot found a groove. Then his hand gripped a knot of pine root. Higher. Higher.

A falcon cried in the distance. Below him, the men waited.

Elias reached the first ledge, heart hammering. He froze and listened. Nothing.

A few more feet. Then he was above the ridge. A flat shelf with scrubby grass and open sky. He lay flat and scanned the treeline.

Two shapes emerged. Sentries—just like before. One smoked a pipe. The other shifted and yawned.

Elias ducked back. He gave the signal: two sharp bird calls, spaced a few seconds apart.

Jonas came next. Then Joseph. Then Abram.

The four crouched behind rocks, rifles drawn.

Elias whispered, "They're not alert."

Jonas's smile was thin. "They will be."

The final hours before dawn ticked by. The men on the bluff huddled in silence, breaths misting into the cold. Below, the camp still flickered with small, dying fires. Elias felt the stillness return—the same eerie waiting he'd felt before—but now it was theirs. Now it was a blade turned outward.

When the signal was given—when the rest of the Overmountain force moved through the woods—this bluff would become the hammer.

Jonas turned to Elias and nodded. "You've got the shot. First volley's yours."

Elias's throat went dry. "You sure?"

"You saw them first. You earned it."

He nodded, pressing himself lower behind the stone.

Far below, a fire flared. A horn blew. The forest cracked with motion.

Then came the scream of warning—Loyalists scrambling.

Elias aimed, heart steady now. He fired.

The battle began.

The first shot echoed like thunder through the mountains.

Elias had barely felt the trigger break beneath his finger when the Loyalist sentry's body jerked and collapsed, pipe still smoldering beside his twitching hand. For a moment—just one—the forest was stunned into silence.

Then it erupted.

Rifles fired from every angle as the Overmountain Men burst through the lower woods. Muzzle flashes lit the trees in brief, violent blinks of fire. Loyalists scrambled out of tents and lean-tos, some with half-fastened belts, others barefoot and fumbling with powder horns. Their surprise was total.

From the ridge above, Elias worked the rifle like Jonas had taught him— breathe, aim, squeeze, reload. The scent of sulfur clung to his skin. He fired again and again, each shot kicking into his shoulder, each target a shape rather than a man. But he could feel it: this was no drill, no game, no hunt.

They were killing.

And he was part of it.

Beside him, Abram let out a whoop, reloading with astonishing speed. Joseph stayed focused, calling out positions and movement below, guiding the riflemen's fire. Jonas, ever quiet, never wasted a bullet. Each shot he took found its mark with frightening efficiency.

A Loyalist captain rallied a knot of men below and tried to lead a charge toward the bluff. Elias dropped one of them before they reached halfway. The others broke and ran, their panic widening the Overmountain advantage.

But it wasn't one-sided for long.

From the treeline near the north slope, Loyalist reinforcements appeared— rifles blazing. They poured into the lower edge of the gulch, and suddenly the tide shifted. Sevier's line staggered under the weight of their volleys. A few

Overmountain men went down hard, rifles clattering from their grip, blood staining the leaves.

Jonas barked to Joseph, "We're not just picking off runners anymore—cover them!"

Elias adjusted his aim, sweeping toward the cluster of Loyalists with the best cover. His breath caught when he saw a young boy—no older than sixteen—fire a musket from behind a stump. The boy's face was smeared with ash, eyes wide and feral. Elias hesitated.

His rifle dipped.

Then Joseph fired past him, and the boy fell like a sack of grain.

"Don't flinch," Joseph snapped. "If they shoot, they die."

Elias swallowed bile and turned back to his sight.

The truth of it slammed into him harder than recoil ever could—this wasn't just bravery and banners. It was smoke, blood, cries in the brush, bodies falling in silence. No glory. Just chaos.

Below, the fighting turned savage. Knives were drawn, and men fell into grappling, choking each other over tree roots and broken rifles. The smoke was thick now—blinding. Someone had set fire to a wagon, and the blaze raced through dry pine needles like a devil's finger.

Elias saw one Overmountain man—bare-chested, bleeding from a gash in the shoulder—tackle a Loyalist into the fire. They both screamed.

"Time to move," Jonas barked.

"What?" Elias turned, heart still pounding.

"They're flanking the ridge. If we stay, we die."

Sure enough, musket balls began pinging off rocks behind them. A second group of Loyalists had climbed the opposite rise and were trying to catch the bluff defenders in a pincer.

Abram cursed as a bullet sliced the air beside his head.

Jonas grabbed Elias's arm. "Come on! Down the side. We regroup behind the lower pines!"

They scrambled backward—sliding, ducking, half-running along the natural curve of the bluff. Abram fired once more and then sprinted with the others. Elias tripped but Joseph caught him, dragging him to cover behind a cluster of thick cedars.

Below, the Overmountain Men had begun to reform. Sevier was pulling his line together, shouting commands over the din. Caleb appeared near the edge of a burned tent, rallying three others with him.

Elias watched as the battle shifted again. What had begun as a surprise attack now devolved into a brutal standoff—neither side yielding. Smoke rolled like fog over the ridge. The crack of rifles had become constant.

Abram leaned against a tree, blood trickling from a cut on his scalp. "Ain't like shooting rabbits," he muttered.

Elias nodded numbly. His mouth was dry as dust.

Jonas reloaded and surveyed the slope. "We've got to collapse their flank. We push in from the side while Sevier drives the front. Split 'em."

Joseph turned to Elias. "You still breathing?"

Elias nodded.

"Then let's earn that breath."

The four of them moved like wolves, hugging the trees, using every shadow and root to mask their path. A dozen paces ahead, they spotted a cluster of Loyalists using overturned barrels and brush for a makeshift barricade.

"Riflemen," Jonas whispered. "They'll pin Sevier's line if we don't break it."

"I count five," Joseph said. "Six, maybe."

"Then we hit hard and fast," Jonas said. "Abram, you toss the flash. Elias and I follow. Joseph covers the rear."

Abram dug into his pouch and produced a homemade firepot—an old flask filled with powder and wrapped in canvas. He lit the fuse with a spark stone and waited two beats.

Then he hurled it.

The explosion was more flash than fire, but it did the trick. The Loyalists shouted and scattered, some stumbling from the blast. Jonas and Elias charged in before the smoke cleared.

Elias didn't think—he simply moved.

His boot hit a loose stone, he ducked beneath a rifle swing, slammed into one man's ribs with his shoulder. A musket fired past his ear. Then he was wrestling on the ground with someone twice his size, struggling for the knife in his belt.

The man had a scar down one cheek and teeth like rotted corn. He snarled and drove a fist into Elias's side. Elias gasped, fought back with every ounce of panic in him, then found the blade.

He stabbed once—twice.

The man went limp.

Elias rolled off him, coughing, chest heaving. Blood smeared his hands.

He stared at them, at the mess he'd made, and nearly vomited.

Then Jonas pulled him up. "We're clear!"

The barricade was theirs.

Joseph ran up moments later, dragging Abram, who was limping from a twisted ankle. "They're falling back!"

Indeed, the Loyalist line was unraveling. The ridge had failed them. The bluff had turned. Sevier's men pushed with renewed fury. Shelby and Campbell's wings tightened their grip.

One last shot rang out across the field.

Then the silence came.

Not peaceful. Not pure. But the kind of silence born only when the dead outnumber the living.

The woods were thick with bodies. Smoke curled from shattered fire pits and scattered supplies. The cries of the wounded punctuated the stillness.

Elias stood in the middle of the wreckage, his arms limp at his sides, staring at the blood on his blade.

Jonas came beside him and said nothing. He didn't have to.

Joseph knelt beside a fallen Overmountain man and closed his eyes. "We'll count soon," he murmured. "But not yet."

Sevier approached the bluff with a handful of surviving riflemen. His face was soot-streaked, eyes burning with pride and grief. "You boys turned the storm," he said simply.

Elias barely heard him. The ringing in his ears hadn't stopped.

Later, as dusk fell again, the survivors began to bury the dead. The ground was too hard in places, so some were wrapped in cloaks and laid beneath pine boughs. Loyalist and patriot alike—none spared the work.

Elias helped lift a man he didn't know. His hands trembled, but he did it anyway.

Jonas watched from a distance, arms folded.

Caleb found them near nightfall. "No word from Ferguson yet," he said. "But they'll know we're coming now."

Elias finally spoke. "They already did."

Caleb nodded. "And we showed them what that means."

That night, the camp was quiet—not with fear, but with something harder. A weight. A reckoning.

Jonas handed Elias a tin cup of water and sat down beside him. "You fought well."

Elias looked at him. "I killed someone."

Jonas didn't flinch. "You'll carry it. Always. But you also saved Joseph. Saved others."

"I still see his face," Elias said. "Every time I close my eyes."

"That's how you know you haven't lost your soul."

Elias turned away, the stars blurring overhead.

Stay strong. Do right. Come back with your soul.

He didn't know if he had. Not anymore.

But he knew one thing: this war wasn't just about land or flags. It was about moments like these—bloody, bitter, and burning into the heart.

And he would not turn back now.

Chapter 7

The smoke had cleared by morning, but the stench lingered—sulfur, blood, and sweat hanging thick in the mist that rolled low through the trees.

Elias stood over a shallow grave, shovel in hand, mud caked to his boots and fingers blistered raw. His shirt clung to his back, soaked in dew and ash. The makeshift cemetery stretched across a slope where the ridge thinned—just enough earth to turn with what tools they had. The dirt was stubborn, clumped with rocks and the roots of the mountain, as if the land itself resisted letting these men go.

He had buried four men that morning. Only one had a name he recognized: Jeb Crowley. A tall, laughing man with a crooked tooth and a fondness for riddles. Elias had spoken with him just two days ago, both of them chewing jerky near the fire. Jeb had taught Elias a trick for re-wrapping his feet at night to avoid frostbite. Now, Jeb lay beneath a bed of pine needles and silence.

The fifth grave was for the enemy.

Elias watched as two men—one limping, the other with a bandaged arm—lowered a Loyalist officer into the pit. No words were said. No prayer offered. Just dirt.

Jonas approached, brushing soot from his sleeves. "That's the last of them?"

Elias nodded.

"You did right by them."

"I don't feel like it."

Jonas didn't push. He squatted near the grave and pressed one hand to the earth. "It never gets easier," he said. "You just learn to carry it better."

Elias dropped the shovel and sat on a log, fingers trembling. The memory of the man he'd killed wouldn't leave him. He could see the man's eyes—wide, surprised, almost human in the final seconds. His body had crumpled like something hollow, not like the solid, living thing it had been just a heartbeat before.

"I didn't even know his name."

"You think he knew yours?" Jonas asked quietly.

Elias shook his head. "That makes it worse somehow. Like we're ghosts passing each other on a battlefield."

Jonas was quiet for a while. Then he said, "Every man we face has a mother, or a child, or someone waiting who won't ever see them again. That's the truth of it. War's not stories—it's a thousand people learning how to live with the hole someone else left behind."

They sat in silence, birds beginning to stir in the branches above. The mountain air, though fresh, felt heavier than it had before. As if the earth itself was mourning.

Joseph joined them with a tin cup of black coffee. "Sevier's calling for a council," he said. "Wants to move before noon."

"Smart," Jonas said. "Ferguson won't sit still. He knows we're coming."

Joseph passed the cup to Elias, who took it without speaking.

Caleb arrived moments later, mud streaked on his coat and a dark smear under his eye. "Scouts say Ferguson's pulling toward Cowpens. He's got Loyalist militias from the South joining him. Could be a thousand strong soon."

"A thousand?" Joseph muttered. "We've got maybe nine hundred now, and half of 'em can barely walk."

"Doesn't matter," Caleb said. "We're still going."

Elias looked up. "Why? After everything...why keep chasing him?"

Caleb's voice didn't rise, but there was steel in it. "Because Ferguson told the Carolinas he'd hang every rebel, burn every home, and leave the women crying over ashes. Because we promised to stop him."

Jonas gave a single nod. "And we keep promises."

Even when they cost you blood.

The company moved by noon.

What remained of the Overmountain force was quieter than it had been in days. No boasts, no laughter. Even Abram—still limping from a twisted ankle—walked in silence, one hand resting on Elias's shoulder for balance. The line of men stretched through the woods like a frayed ribbon of resolve.

Elias kept to the middle of the line. He didn't want to see the rear—where the wounded walked slowly and the empty places marked the dead. And he didn't want to lead either.

He just wanted to walk and forget.

But forgetting wasn't so easy.

They passed the site of the battle by late afternoon. Smoke still curled from a charred wagon. Crows circled overhead, and Elias didn't dare look long at the fields where the bodies had lain. The breeze carried a sourness he'd never known before—a clinging, iron scent of spilled life.

They stopped briefly to allow the rear to catch up. Elias sat on a stone and removed his boots to wring out his socks, hands shaking. A boy his age named Daniel from the Carter contingent sat beside him, arms wrapped around his knees.

"I can't sleep," Daniel murmured. "Every time I close my eyes, I hear them again. Screaming."

Elias hesitated, then said, "You're not alone."

Daniel nodded. "Is it supposed to feel like this?"

"No," Elias said softly. "But it does."

By evening, they reached the base of a wide, muddy stream.

Joseph waded in first, boots splashing, rifle held high. "Not deep," he called. "But cold as a Tory's heart."

Elias followed, breath catching at the icy bite of the water. On the far bank, men built camp slowly—no fire unless covered, no talking unless necessary. Scouts warned that Ferguson's pickets could be anywhere now.

Elias sat beside Jonas beneath a gnarled chestnut tree. His boots steamed faintly as they dried by a covered ember-bed. The flicker of firelight didn't warm him so much as remind him he was still alive.

"What happens if we don't catch him?" Elias asked.

Jonas didn't answer right away. "Then he burns more towns. Hangs more men. And next spring, they call it a Loyalist victory."

"You really think we can stop him?"

Jonas looked at the firelight reflecting in Elias's eyes. "You already have."

"How?"

"You didn't run," he said simply. "That's how it starts."

Abram limped over and dropped beside them with a groan. "Still hurts like fire, but I ain't dead. So that's something."

Joseph chuckled. "You're too stubborn to die."

"Maybe," Abram said. "But this ain't how I pictured it going. Thought we'd have won by now. Go home. Tell stories. Kiss my sweetheart and say I was brave."

Elias looked into the fire. "We're still writing them."

The men nodded in silence. Around them, the night deepened. Someone began softly humming a tune—low, mournful, and familiar, like a cradle song sung for the dead.

They fell into a fitful sleep beneath a sky painted with bruised clouds and a sliver of moon. The wind howled that night—not the kind that chills, but the kind that remembers.

And somewhere in the dark, Elias dreamed of Samuel again—standing atop a smoky ridge, looking down at him with both pride and sorrow in his eyes.

The rain came at dawn—soft at first, like fingers tapping against canvas, then harder, a steady, cold percussion on the leaves above. Elias woke beneath his cloak, teeth chattering, the sound of dripping water tapping in time with the ache in his limbs.

They broke camp before sunrise.

The men moved slowly, bedrolls soaked, bread soggy in their packs. Muskets were carefully wrapped in oilcloth, but even so, Elias feared for the powder.

Wet flint and damp touchholes meant dead rifles. And if Ferguson turned back on them now, they'd be marching into an ambush armed with little more than knives and grit.

"Keep your packs high," Joseph called, trudging through shin-deep water. "And your wits higher."

The trail wound south through lowland thickets and waterlogged fields. Scouts reported that Ferguson's forces were just a day ahead—maybe less. But the Loyalists were moving faster than expected, buoyed by fresh horses and lighter loads.

"Cowards run easier," Caleb muttered. "Don't need to haul courage when you've none to begin with."

Elias wished he shared the same fire. His legs were leaden. Every step sank into the mud and pulled his strength down with it. He couldn't remember the last time he'd slept without waking from dreams filled with gunshots or Samuel's voice calling from somewhere he couldn't reach.

By midday, they passed the ruins of a Loyalist supply post. Charred barrels and broken wagons littered the clearing. A single boot stuck out of the ashes, melted to the calf of what once had been a soldier.

"Ferguson's covering his trail," Jonas said grimly. "Burning what he can't carry. He doesn't want us gaining a drop of advantage."

They paused only briefly to scavenge. Elias found a mostly dry canteen and a wool glove missing its thumb. Abram found a torn scrap of blue cloth that looked like part of a South Carolina regiment's flag.

"We're getting close," he said, folding it into his coat.

The trail grew narrower as they entered pine forest. Branches bent low with the weight of rain, brushing against the men's faces and shoulders like the mountain itself was trying to turn them back.

"You think Ferguson's headed to King's Mountain?" Elias asked, sloshing beside Jonas.

"He wants the high ground," Jonas answered. "That ridge would give him an edge. And he's got friends there—Tory strongholds scattered through the hills."

Joseph caught up, lowering his voice. "Word is, Ferguson's sending riders to call in Loyalist reinforcements. If they reach him in time, we'll be outnumbered two-to-one."

Jonas scowled. "Then we have to reach him first."

That night, they camped in a hollow, the rain still falling in sheets. There was no dry ground to speak of. Elias spread his blanket on a patch of pine needles and sat back against a fallen log, boots off, toes white and wrinkled from cold.

Across the firepit, Abram was fiddling with a snare he'd set earlier. "Caught a rabbit," he said. "Scrawny thing, but better than chewing on moldy bread."

Joseph smiled. "You saying that loaf I gave you was moldy?"

"I'm saying it walked away on its own."

The others chuckled—brief, exhausted sounds—but laughter all the same. Elias leaned back and let it wash over him, like a wave that reminded him he wasn't entirely hollow inside.

Later, Jonas handed him a folded note, the edges spotted with water.

"What's this?" Elias asked.

"From Captain McDowell," Jonas said. "Wants a runner at dawn to alert the other companies. You're fast and quiet."

Elias hesitated. "How far?"

"Three miles down the ridge, then follow the west branch of the creek. You'll know the camp when you see smoke—if they're still there."

Elias tucked the note into his shirt. "I'll go."

"Don't wait for permission," Jonas added. "And don't take the main trail— Tories might be watching it."

That night, Elias barely slept. The rain slowed to a drizzle, but his bones still ached, and the silence between storms was louder than the thunder itself. He rose before the others, tying on his boots with numb fingers and slipping into the trees like a shadow.

The forest at dawn was a world untouched. Mist hung low over the creek, and every leaf gleamed with rain. Birds had yet to wake, and even the wind seemed to hold its breath.

Elias moved quickly, weaving through underbrush, his moccasins squishing with each step. He stayed off the trail, crossing deer paths and sliding down slick banks to avoid open sightlines. Twice he stopped, heart thudding, when the cry of a hawk pierced the morning quiet. But no musket fire followed.

An hour later, he saw smoke curling between the trees.

The camp was smaller than expected—just fifteen men huddled around a tarp, cooking something over coals that smelled faintly of spoiled meat. A young lieutenant spotted Elias first, musket half-raised.

"Don't shoot," Elias said quickly, raising both hands.

"Name and company!"

"Elias McCrae, under Captain Gillespie. I've got orders from McDowell."

The tension broke, and the men relaxed slightly. Elias delivered the note, waited while it was read, and accepted a biscuit and a seat by the fire while they packed up.

"You've seen Ferguson's men?" one soldier asked him.

"Not directly. Just burned wagons and dead Loyalists."

"Well," the lieutenant muttered, "then you've seen the truth."

Elias stayed only as long as necessary, then turned back. The mist had thickened. He retraced his steps, listening to the squelch of his own footfalls and the echo of water dripping from the canopy above.

When he neared the main ridge, he paused.

A horse.

The sound was faint—just ahead and downhill, past a screen of birch trees. He dropped to his belly and crawled forward, peering through the wet brush.

A single rider, wrapped in a cloak, was picking through the trail. British saddle. Blue sash. The man glanced over his shoulder, nerves twitching in every line of his posture.

A courier.

Elias's heart hammered. If he could stop that rider...

He crept closer, musket tight in his grip. The rider paused to adjust his reins, and Elias rose halfway—aimed—and froze.

What if he missed?

What if others were nearby?

A snap of a branch behind him made the decision for him. He fired.

The musket cracked through the forest, startling a flock of birds into flight.

The rider jerked—then slumped forward in the saddle. The horse reared and bolted into the trees, dragging the body for several yards before the weight tumbled loose.

Elias didn't breathe until the silence returned.

He waited five minutes—ten—then crept down to the body. A young man, maybe twenty, a satchel slung over his shoulder. The bullet had taken him through the chest. Elias pried the bag open with shaking fingers.

Inside: maps. Sealed letters. A small, rolled flag with Ferguson's personal mark.

Orders.

He gathered what he could, stuffed it inside his shirt, and ran.

By the time he reached the Overmountain camp, the sun had broken through the clouds. The air steamed from trees like breath from the earth. Men turned to him as he entered, mud-caked and wild-eyed.

"I found him," Elias gasped. "A courier. I have his papers."

Jonas took the satchel and scanned the contents. His expression shifted from confusion to fire. "He's headed to King's Mountain. And he's expecting reinforcements within three days."

Joseph stepped forward. "Then we have two days to stop him."

Caleb's voice rang out clear: "Pack everything. We move now."

Elias sat down on a stump, panting. His muscles burned. His mind raced. But something new had kindled inside him.

A flicker of purpose.

Of momentum.

For the first time since the battle, the Overmountain Men weren't just reacting.

They were chasing.

The rain thinned to a steady drizzle as Elias and Josiah pushed through the dense underbrush, the scent of damp earth thick in the air. Overhead, the heavy gray clouds drifted, occasionally revealing faint slivers of light, but the sky remained a heavy dome that pressed down on them. The forest was alive with muted sounds — the drip of water from pine needles, the distant cry of a raven, the scuffle of boots on muddy ground.

Elias glanced over at Josiah, who had stopped to catch his breath, wiping rain from his face. His eyes, usually so full of mischief and fire, were drawn and shadowed with worry.

"You feeling it too?" Elias asked quietly.

Josiah nodded slowly. "Yeah. It's like the land's holding its breath. You can smell it, feel it in your bones. Something's coming."

The men around them were quieter than usual, voices hushed and clipped as they moved in tighter formation. The weight of the chase was wearing down even the toughest among them. Joseph rode ahead, scanning the horizon, the ever-watchful captain who bore the burden of every decision.

Elias shifted the satchel of stolen Loyalist orders against his chest. The papers inside were soaked but intact, a tangible reminder of the urgency that gripped them all. Those orders meant reinforcements — fresh troops, better supplies — would soon swell Ferguson's ranks. Time was running out.

"Do you think we can catch him before the others arrive?" Elias asked Josiah, his voice low, almost a whisper.

Josiah shrugged, eyes fixed on the muddy trail ahead. "I don't know. But we've got to try. If we don't stop Ferguson now, it won't just be us who pay the price. It'll be the whole mountain, the whole country."

Elias swallowed hard. The truth of Josiah's words settled like a stone in his gut. This wasn't just a fight for their survival — it was a fight for their homes, their families, their very way of life.

As they trudged deeper into the woods, the trail narrowed, forcing them single file. The trees pressed in tight, their twisted roots tangled like the doubts twisting in Elias's mind. Every snap of a twig, every rustle of leaves, set his heart pounding. The forest seemed to watch, silent and waiting.

Ahead, the flicker of a campfire's glow shone through the trees. The men slowed, weapons ready, eyes sharp. They approached cautiously, the firelight dancing over grim faces as men prepared for the night. Elias recognized the soldiers as part of Captain McDowell's company, weary but resolute.

Joseph's voice cut through the damp night air. "We move at first light. Rest now."

Elias dropped his pack beside the fire, the damp cloth clinging cold against his skin. He sank to the ground, exhaustion threatening to drag him under, but sleep wouldn't come. Not yet.

Nearby, Caleb and Abram sat sharpening their knives, their murmured conversation a fragile thread of normalcy in the tension.

"Think Ferguson knows we're this close?" Elias asked, voice barely audible.

Caleb's jaw tightened. "If he does, he's too smart to show it. But he's got to feel the heat. He knows we're hunting him, just like we are wolves after a wounded deer."

Abram chuckled darkly. "Hope that deer's got some fight left in it."

The fire crackled, embers swirling upward like sparks of hope. Elias gazed into the flames, thinking of Samuel — his brother, gone but never far from his thoughts. The memory of Samuel's steady voice, his unwavering courage, kindled a fierce warmth inside Elias's chest.

He wasn't just fighting for himself anymore.

He was fighting for Samuel.

For their family.

For the promise of a free mountain.

Night deepened, and the camp settled into restless sleep. Elias lay back, eyes tracing the canopy above, the rain now a gentle patter, a lullaby for warriors waiting for dawn.

But sleep was elusive. Instead, his mind raced with plans, fears, and the unspoken questions between the men — questions about loyalty, courage, and the cost of what they were about to face.

In the quiet darkness, a whispered conversation floated nearby.

"I don't trust those Tory boys," Josiah said. "They'll break like dry twigs when the firing starts."

Joseph's steady voice replied, "Maybe. But we all have our breaking points."

Caleb added, "It's not just about who breaks first. It's about who stands last."

Elias clenched his fists, feeling the fire between them — not just the one in the campfire, but the fire that bound them all: anger, fear, hope, and an unyielding will to stand against tyranny.

Dawn crept slowly, gray and cold. The men stirred, gathering their weapons, checking powder and musket balls with trembling fingers. Elias felt the tension coil tighter in his belly.

Joseph called the men together. "This is the moment. The battle ahead will decide everything. Remember why we fight — for our homes, our families, and the freedom we've sworn to keep. Stay close, watch each other's backs, and hold the line."

Elias met the eyes of those around him — young men, hardened fighters, all bound by a common purpose. He swallowed his fear, feeling the fire grow inside.

They moved out, the woods echoing with the sound of boots and whispered prayers. The long wait was over. The fire between them was burning bright.

The clash had ended, but the forest was still thick with the acrid smoke of spent muskets. The air hung heavy, smelling of burnt powder and damp earth. Men moved sluggishly, many leaning on their rifles for support, faces streaked with dirt, sweat, and blood. Some groaned in pain, others sat silently, staring blankly at the canopy overhead.

Elias lowered his musket slowly, feeling the sting in his shoulder where the bullet had grazed him. The pain was sharp but bearable — a burning reminder of how close he had come to falling. His breath came uneven, chest rising and falling with the weight of exhaustion and adrenaline.

He looked around and saw Josiah sitting against a tree, wiping a cut on his cheek with a bloodied cloth. Caleb was bent over a fallen comrade, trying to staunch the flow of blood from a deep wound. Abram paced near the edge of their small clearing, the tension in his shoulders unbroken despite the battle's end.

Joseph stood at the center of the camp, barking orders to organize the wounded and gather what supplies they could salvage. His voice was tired but resolute. Elias admired his captain's unwavering spirit — it kept the men focused and moving, even when the victory tasted bittersweet.

Elias staggered toward Joseph. "Captain... what now?"

Joseph glanced at him, then nodded toward a group of scouts returning from the ridge. "Ferguson's forces are retreating, but reinforcements are rumored to be on the way. We can't rest yet. We need to prepare for another fight — or a pursuit."

Elias swallowed hard, the reality settling in. The battle was just the beginning.

Josiah limped over, his face pale but determined. "You sure you're alright?"

Elias touched his shoulder. "It's just a scratch. Nothing I can't handle."

Josiah smiled grimly. "Good. We'll need you."

As they began to set up a makeshift camp, Elias found a quiet moment to think. The faces of those lost in battle flickered in his mind — friends, strangers, all united by a cause larger than themselves. The fire between them had burned bright, but at a heavy cost.

He crouched beside a fallen oak, fingers tracing the rough bark, seeking comfort in the steady presence of the woods. The war had changed everything — the innocence of youth, the certainty of tomorrow. But amid the chaos, Elias felt a stubborn hope, a resolve that wouldn't be broken.

Caleb approached, breaking the silence. "We did what we came to do. Ferguson's plans are scattered now. We've slowed him down."

Elias nodded. "But for how long?"

Abram joined them. "Long enough for the mountain to rise. For us to stand."

The men shared a brief, quiet moment — the unspoken bond of those who had fought side by side.

Night fell again, colder this time, but the campfires burned steady, casting long shadows that danced like ghosts among the trees. Elias sat beside Josiah, their conversation low and reflective.

"Do you think it's really over?" Elias asked.

Josiah shook his head. "No. Not yet. But every victory is a step closer."

Elias glanced at the stars peeking through the branches. Somewhere out there, Samuel's spirit felt near — a guiding flame in the darkness.

"We'll keep the fire alive," Elias said softly.

Josiah grinned. "That's the spirit."

The night stretched on, the mountain quiet but vigilant. Tomorrow would bring new challenges — new battles, new sacrifices. But for now, the fire between them smoldered, a promise of strength and unity against the coming storm.

The dawn came slow, shrouded in mist that clung to the trees like a thin veil, muting the colors of the forest. Elias awoke stiff and sore, the dull ache in his shoulder a constant reminder of yesterday's battle. Around the camp, men stirred quietly, rubbing sleep from their eyes, tending to wounds, and readying their gear.

Joseph stood near a rough map laid across a makeshift table—an old tree stump. His finger traced lines that cut across valleys and ridges, marking the positions of their men and those of the enemy. The flicker of a nearby fire cast shadows on his face, hardening his expression.

"We've bought ourselves some time," Joseph said as Elias approached. "But we can't linger. Ferguson won't be idle for long."

Caleb joined them, his face drawn but determined. "Our scouts reported movement east. Reinforcements could arrive by nightfall."

Elias frowned, the weight of their precarious position pressing down on him. "What's the plan?"

Joseph looked at each man in turn. "We rest briefly, then we move out. We'll take the ridge north of here—higher ground gives us the advantage. We need to slow Ferguson's advance before he regroups."

Josiah, limping but steady, added, "We split into two groups. One holds the ridge; the other disrupts their supply lines below."

Elias listened, absorbing every detail. The strategy felt sound, but uncertainty gnawed at him. The men were tired, and many wounded, but the fight wasn't over.

After the meeting dispersed, Elias found a quiet spot beneath a towering pine. He pulled a small piece of parchment from his pack—the last letter from Samuel. His fingers trembled as he read the words again:

"Hold fast to what you believe, Elias. The fire we carry is brighter than any darkness."

A flicker of warmth rose within him despite the cold morning. Samuel's faith was a steady flame, guiding him through fear and doubt.

Suddenly, footsteps approached. Josiah sat down beside him, wincing slightly. "You okay?"

Elias nodded, folding the letter carefully. "I will be. Just thinking."

Josiah's gaze drifted toward the distant hills. "Every time I think about home, about what we're fighting for... it steels me. But it also scares me."

"Me too," Elias admitted. "I never thought war would be like this. So raw, so close."

Josiah chuckled softly. "It changes a man. Makes you see things in black and white — and shades of gray you never expected."

Elias looked into his friend's eyes and saw the truth there. This fight was more than muskets and marching; it was about survival, identity, and the ties that bound them to something greater.

"Do you think we'll make it through?" Elias asked quietly.

Josiah's answer was simple: "We have to. For Samuel, for the mountains, for all of us."

The camp slowly came alive as the sun pushed through the mist, casting long beams of light that warmed the chill of the morning air. Men shared whispered conversations, some tending to makeshift bandages while others scavenged for fresh water or prepared meager breakfasts. The wounds from the previous day were a stark reminder of the cost paid, and yet there was an unspoken resolve threading through the camp.

Elias helped Caleb collect firewood, his mind drifting between the immediate tasks and the heavy weight of command decisions that Joseph and the others had laid out. The plan to split their forces was bold — the ridge offered a defensible position, but leaving the supply lines vulnerable was a risk they had no choice but to take.

Later, as the groups prepared to move out, Joseph called Elias over. "You're with me on the ridge," Joseph said, "I want you sharp. Your eyes and instincts will be vital."

Elias nodded, feeling both honor and pressure settle on his shoulders. He looked over to Josiah, who gave a subtle nod of encouragement despite the limp that slowed his step.

The climb to the ridge was grueling, the ground uneven and slick from last night's rain. As they ascended, Elias glanced back at the camp, now a small cluster of tents and fires nestled among the trees. Behind them, the forest seemed calm, but Elias knew the quiet was only temporary.

At the summit, the view stretched endlessly — rolling hills dotted with patches of forest, winding rivers glinting like silver threads in the morning sun. From this vantage point, the enemy's movements could be tracked, their supply lines vulnerable.

Joseph gathered the men into a loose formation, the murmurs of preparation punctuated by the clinking of weapons and the rustling of gear. Elias steadied his breath, fingers tightening around his musket.

Hours passed as they watched, waiting, eyes scanning every shadow, every flicker of movement. The silence was thick, heavy with anticipation.

Suddenly, a scout signaled from the west, urgently motioning. Joseph's gaze sharpened.

"They're moving," he whispered. "Ferguson's men are pushing forward — supply wagons included."

The tension snapped taut. Joseph barked orders to intercept, and Elias's heart hammered as they moved swiftly down the ridge to intercept the supply convoy.

The ambush was swift and brutal. Men dashed from behind trees and rocks, muskets firing, voices shouting war cries. The clash was chaotic, raw — a deadly dance of smoke, blood, and shouts.

Elias fought fiercely, muscles burning, ears ringing with the cacophony. He caught a glimpse of Josiah across the fray, rallying men despite the pain that slowed him. Together, they pushed forward, the supply wagons seized and destroyed.

When the dust settled, the men counted their spoils and tended to the wounded. The victory was hard-won, but it disrupted Ferguson's advance — buying precious time.

As night fell once more, Elias sat by a fire with Joseph and Josiah, the quiet hum of the forest surrounding them. The weight of the day pressed on him, but so did a fierce pride.

Joseph broke the silence. "This isn't just a battle. It's a test of endurance, spirit."

Josiah nodded. "And we're not done yet."

Elias looked up at the stars, feeling the fire within burn brighter than ever. No matter the darkness ahead, the mountains and their people would stand strong.

The camp settled into an uneasy quiet as the embers of the fire flickered low. The men, exhausted from the day's ambush, moved with heavy limbs, their faces marked by grime and fatigue. Some gathered around the warmth of the fire, sharing sparse rations and quiet words, while others sought the solitude of the trees to tend to wounds or steal a moment's rest.

Elias sat beside Josiah, his fingers tracing the worn leather of his pack as his thoughts churned. The battle had tested more than just their strength — it had revealed the depth of their resolve, the fragile thread holding them together. He could still hear the echo of musket fire in his mind, the cries of men fighting not just for survival, but for something sacred.

Josiah broke the silence. "You holding up, Elias?"

He nodded slowly. "I am. But it's more than that. I feel like... I don't know... like I'm carrying more than just a musket."

Josiah gave a tired smile. "That's the weight of this war, brother. It's heavy. But it shapes us, too."

Nearby, Caleb tended to a wounded soldier, his hands steady despite the blood. Elias admired his calm — a pillar amid chaos. Abram was sharpening his blade, eyes distant, lost in thought. The firelight caught the lines of worry etched on his face.

Suddenly, a scout burst into camp, breathless and wide-eyed. "Captain! We've got trouble. A patrol from Ferguson's men spotted near the northern creek. They're moving fast."

Joseph stood immediately, voice sharp. "Sound the alarms. We move at first light."

The men sprang into action, the calm replaced by urgent preparation. Elias felt the familiar surge of adrenaline — the fire within roaring back to life.

As night deepened, Elias found himself pacing near the edge of the camp, the cool air brushing against his skin. He thought of Samuel again — his brother's courage, the letters filled with hope and determination. Elias whispered a silent vow to carry that spirit forward, no matter the cost.

The hours passed slowly until dawn crept over the horizon, painting the sky with soft hues of pink and gold. The men assembled, weary but ready. Joseph outlined the new plan: intercept the patrol before it could alert the main force.

Elias rode with Josiah and Caleb, the three men sharing a quiet determination. The forest was alive with early morning sounds — birdsong, rustling leaves, the distant murmur of running water.

Suddenly, Josiah raised a hand, signaling to halt. Ahead, through the thicket, they glimpsed the enemy patrol — a small group moving cautiously along the creek bank.

The ambush was swift. Using the terrain to their advantage, Elias and his companions closed in silently, catching the patrol off guard. The fight was brief but fierce; a few muskets fired, blades flashed, and then silence fell once more.

As the patrol surrendered, Elias's chest swelled with pride and relief. Each victory, no matter how small, was a step toward the freedom they sought.

Back at camp, the men treated their prisoners with wary respect — a reminder that even in war, honor must endure.

That night, as Elias wrote a letter to his mother by firelight, he poured his heart onto the page, sharing the weight of the fight and the hope that sustained him.

The fire crackled softly as Elias sealed the letter, the wax impression still warm in his palm. He folded the paper carefully, tucking it into his pack alongside Samuel's letter. The two missives were bridges between past and present, reminders of everything he fought for—and everything he feared he might lose.

Nearby, Josiah approached, his limp still noticeable but his step lighter. "You're doing good work, Elias. Your words—your spirit—they matter."

Elias looked up, surprised by the quiet encouragement. "Sometimes I wonder if it's enough."

Josiah's eyes held steady. "Enough? Maybe not yet. But every story we tell, every fight we wage—it builds something larger. Something lasting."

The camp was alive with quiet energy, men tending to muskets and patching torn clothing. Caleb joined them, wiping sweat from his brow, his usually steady hands trembling slightly.

"Caleb?" Elias asked. "You alright?"

Caleb shook his head slowly. "I'm just... thinking about what's ahead. This isn't a skirmish anymore. It's a war."

The words hung heavy in the cool night air. Elias swallowed hard. The weight of the truth pressed in — the fight for freedom was more dangerous, more complex than he'd imagined.

Suddenly, Joseph called the men together. His voice cut through the night like a blade, sharp and commanding. "Tomorrow we move deeper into the mountains. Intelligence reports a larger force gathering near the river. We must strike first or risk being overwhelmed."

A murmur rippled through the crowd. The stakes had risen. The mountain air felt colder, the shadows deeper.

That night, Elias lay beneath the stars, the familiar constellations offering little comfort. He thought of his family, of Samuel's words echoing in his mind. The fire within flickered—sometimes bright, sometimes dim—but never extinguished.

Morning came quickly. The men broke camp with practiced efficiency, hearts steeled for what lay ahead. As they marched toward the river, Elias felt the pulse of the land beneath his feet—the ancient strength of the mountains, silent witnesses to their struggle.

At the river's edge, the soldiers paused. The water rushed cold and clear, a sharp contrast to the tension in the air. Scouts reported the enemy camp just beyond the tree line, fires burning bright in the growing dusk.

Joseph gathered the men. "This will be our most dangerous fight yet. But it's also our chance to cripple Ferguson's forces and turn the tide."

Elias's pulse quickened. The fire inside him blazed fiercely as the men prepared for battle.

They moved quietly through the trees, shadows among shadows. The scent of pine and damp earth filled the air. The enemy camp lay just ahead, their movements visible in flickering firelight.

The ambush was swift and brutal. Muskets cracked in the night, men shouted and clashed. Elias fought with everything he had, each breath burning in his lungs.

In the chaos, he spotted Josiah, bloodied but unyielding, fighting side by side with Caleb. The bond between them was a lifeline, a reminder of what they fought for.

As dawn broke, the enemy's lines began to falter. The mountain warriors pressed their advantage, driving Ferguson's men back into retreat.

The victory was hard-earned and costly. Elias knelt beside a fallen comrade, the weight of loss settling heavy on his heart.

Yet in the rising sun, he found hope — a fragile, fierce hope that their fire would one day light the way to freedom.

Chapter 8

A cold, pale dawn broke over the camp, while the mountains cast their long, solemn shadows across the damp earth. Elias awoke slowly, the ache in his limbs a dull but persistent reminder of yesterday's battle by the river. He lay still for a moment, listening to the soft murmur of men stirring around the camp. Their movements were slow, measured — weighted by exhaustion and the bitter grief that clung to the air like morning mist.

His body ached in places he hadn't realized could hurt, every muscle tight from fighting, from fear, and from the desperate hope that they had done enough to survive. Yet it was the silence — that long pause between heartbeats and moments — that unsettled him most. The absence of noise where there had once been the roar of muskets and the shouts of men made the world feel strangely hollow.

He rose carefully, trying not to disturb the few still asleep beneath threadbare blankets. The fire from the night before had burned low, reduced to glowing embers, and the faint scent of smoke clung to the air, a reminder of the fierce battle fought and the lives lost.

By the dying fire, Josiah sat hunched, staring into the last flickers of flame. His usual confident bravado was tempered by a deep, hard fatigue and the ghostly memories of comrades who would never rise again. Elias settled beside him quietly.

"Morning," Elias said softly.

Josiah's gaze didn't lift, but he nodded in acknowledgment. "Another day," he murmured, voice rough but steady. "We're still here. That's something."

Elias nodded, feeling the truth behind the words, but also the weight that survival demanded — the cost of every breath taken while others had fallen. Around them, the camp was slowly coming alive. Men tended to wounds with tattered cloth and whatever medicine they had; some shared small bites of stale bread or pieces of dried meat. Caleb moved from soldier to soldier, his calm presence a comfort amid the suffering, his hands steady despite the chaos.

Elias's eyes drifted toward the ridge where the first rays of sunlight pierced through thick pines, scattering golden shafts of light onto the forest floor. His thoughts wandered to Samuel, to the letters that had once filled his pockets with hope and direction. The fire inside him flickered — fragile and trembling — demanding nurture in a world growing ever darker.

The camp was silent except for the soft sounds of morning preparations. The men spoke little, their conversations subdued, broken by whispered prayers and occasional sighs heavy with grief. Joseph stood before them, shoulders squared, voice firm despite the ache he carried beneath the surface.

"We mourn those we've lost," he began, his eyes sweeping across the group. "But we must remember why we fight — for our homes, our families, and the promise of freedom."

A murmur of agreement spread, quiet but resolute. Elias felt those words settle deep in his chest, mingling with the aching loss and the stubborn spark of determination that had carried him this far.

After the sparse breakfast, Elias slipped away from the camp to a quiet spot near the riverbank. The water flowed steadily, cold and clear, rushing over smooth stones without hesitation — indifferent to the turmoil it witnessed. He knelt by the bank, cupping his hands to drink the icy liquid. The coldness shocked his senses and for a moment, he simply breathed, letting the rushing water wash over his fingers and clear his mind.

His thoughts turned inward, drifting like the leaves caught in the gentle current. The faces of fallen comrades floated in his memory — friends lost to the chaos of war, voices echoing in the rustling leaves and distant bird calls. He pressed a hand to his chest, feeling the steady beat beneath his palm, a small but powerful reminder that he was still here to carry their story forward.

Josiah came quietly to sit beside him, his limp barely noticeable in the soft earth. "You're carrying more than your share, Elias," he said quietly.

Elias shook his head, eyes fixed on the river. "I don't know how to carry it all. Sometimes it feels like the weight will crush me. The names, the faces — it's too much."

Josiah's gaze was steady, full of hard-earned wisdom. "You carry it because you must. Because someone has to. But don't forget, you don't have to carry it alone."

Their eyes met, a silent understanding passing between them. The war had forged bonds deeper than blood — a brotherhood born of shared hardship and unwavering loyalty.

As the sun climbed higher, the camp stirred with quiet purpose. Men repaired tattered clothing, sharpened blades, and mended muskets with hands that trembled but refused to stop. The losses of the past battles hung heavy like a dark cloud, but so did the unyielding hope that tomorrow might bring a new dawn.

Elias stood and stretched, the mountain breeze cool against his sweat-damp skin. His gaze swept across the trees, the path ahead uncertain and fraught with danger. Yet, within the deep rhythm of his heart, he found resolve — a promise to fight not just for survival, but for the future Samuel had dreamed of. For freedom. For home.

Back at the fire, a few men huddled close, sharing stories and memories to keep the darkness at bay. Elias joined them briefly, listening to their laughter mingled with sorrow — the fragile balance of life at war.

As the day wore on, Elias's thoughts returned again and again to the faces of those who had fallen, and to the letter Samuel had written — a letter that was no longer just words on paper, but a call to arms, a beacon in the shadow of despair.

The mountain whispered around them, ancient and unyielding, a silent witness to their struggle. Elias clenched his fists, determination settling like stone within him. They would face whatever came next — together.

The camp was beginning to hum with restless energy when a sharp crack in the brush alerted the men. Heads snapped toward the edge of the tree line, muskets raised, fingers tightening around triggers. The tension was palpable—months of battle had taught them that every unexpected sound could mean death.

Out stepped a lone figure, slender but moving with the surety of someone accustomed to the wilderness. He wore a weathered leather coat and a wide-brimmed hat pulled low, shadowing his sharp eyes. His boots, caked with mud, were silent against the soft earth, and a satchel hung at his side, bulging with papers and maps.

"Hold your fire," the stranger called, raising his hands slowly in peace.

Joseph stepped forward, hand resting on the hilt of his sword. "Who are you? What news do you bring?"

The man's eyes flicked over the gathered soldiers before settling on Elias, whose heart suddenly pounded with a mixture of curiosity and unease.

"My name's Caleb Mason. I'm a scout for the militia up north," he said, voice low but steady. "I bring urgent news. The enemy's movements have changed — they're gathering strength, preparing for a push that could break us if we're not ready."

A murmur rippled through the camp. Joseph's jaw tightened as he motioned for the men to lower their weapons.

"Tell us everything," Joseph said.

Caleb pulled a crumpled map from his satchel and spread it on a nearby stump. His fingers traced lines and markings, illustrating the positions of their forces and the enemy's encampments. Elias leaned in, captivated by the sharp detail and precision.

"The British have reinforced their troops near the valley to the east," Caleb explained. "They've also called in loyalists from the southern plantations. We're outnumbered if we don't act carefully."

Elias's mind raced. He'd fought alongside these men for months, seen the horrors of battle, and yet the threat of overwhelming odds was still a bitter pill. The promise of victory seemed to flicker with every new warning.

Caleb's eyes caught Elias's again. "You're not just a fighter, are you?"

Elias blinked, caught off guard.

"Your name's familiar," Caleb continued, voice softening. "I've heard tales of your bravery on the river. You carry more than a musket — you carry hope."

The weight of those words pressed down on Elias's chest. Hope. A fragile thing in times like these. But Caleb's gaze was unwavering, offering a strange comfort.

The men gathered closer, their faces a mixture of fatigue and renewed determination. Caleb spoke of plans—scouting missions, possible ambushes, the need for swift and quiet movements through the forest. His knowledge was vast, born of months tracking the enemy through rugged terrain.

Joseph listened carefully, weighing Caleb's reports against what they already knew. The leaders debated quietly, voices low but firm, balancing risk and strategy.

Elias found himself drawn to Caleb's calm confidence, a stark contrast to the chaos that had engulfed their lives. The scout's presence sparked a flicker of something new—a chance to tip the scales.

As the afternoon sun filtered through the trees, Elias and Caleb walked together along a narrow path, away from the camp's watchful eyes.

"You're not like the others," Caleb said, breaking the silence. "There's fire in you — but also doubt."

Elias nodded, his gaze fixed on the trail ahead. "It's hard not to doubt. Every day feels like a fight just to keep going."

Caleb smiled faintly. "That's what makes you strong. The ones who never lose hope are the ones who carry the war in their bones."

They spoke of their pasts—Caleb's life as a woodsman and messenger, Elias's journey from blacksmith's son to reluctant soldier. Their shared experiences forged a quiet bond, bridging the gap between stranger and comrade.

As they returned to camp, Elias felt a new sense of purpose settle inside him. The road ahead was treacherous, but with allies like Caleb, perhaps the odds could be faced head-on.

Back among the men, whispers of the scout's news spread quickly. The tension remained, but beneath it lay a current of resolve—an unspoken vow that they would stand together, no matter the storm to come.

That night, as Elias lay beneath the stars, the flickering campfires casting shadows on the trees, he allowed himself to hope. For the first time in weeks, the future felt possible—not just a distant dream, but a fragile promise waiting to be seized.

The night deepened, the sky a vast canvas of stars shimmering like distant fires. The camp was quieter now, the usual restless murmurs subdued beneath a heavy blanket of exhaustion. Men huddled close to their small fires, some sharing whispered conversations, others lost in silent thought, clutching memories as tightly as their worn blankets.

Elias sat apart near the edge of the camp, his gaze fixed on the flickering flames. The crackle of burning wood mingled with the faint chorus of night insects and the rustle of leaves stirred by a gentle breeze. Around him, the mountain breathed—ancient and unyielding—a witness to every struggle, every loss, every victory.

His fingers toyed absently with the letter Samuel had written weeks before, its edges soft from constant folding and unfolding. The words still burned within him, a reminder of all he fought for—and all that might never be.

A sudden sound pulled him from his reverie. Footsteps—soft but deliberate—approaching through the shadows. He didn't need to turn to know who it was. Caleb Mason emerged from the darkness, his face half-lit by the firelight, eyes steady and thoughtful.

"Can't sleep?" Caleb asked quietly, settling beside Elias without waiting for an invitation.

Elias shook his head. "Too many thoughts. Too many memories."

Caleb nodded, understanding. "War has a way of filling the mind with ghosts. Sometimes they come to remind us why we fight."

For a long moment, neither spoke. The fire cast their faces in shifting light and shadow, the silence between them comfortable and unforced.

Finally, Elias broke the quiet. "Do you ever wonder if it's all worth it? The blood, the pain, the losses...?"

Caleb's gaze hardened, reflecting a lifetime of hard truths. "Every day. But then I remember what we're fighting for—not just survival, but the chance to live free. To build something better than what we had."

Elias's thoughts drifted to his family, to the small cabin they had left behind and the promise of a future that seemed so fragile now. He wondered if he'd ever see it again, if the war would claim him like it had claimed so many others.

"Sometimes I fear I'm not strong enough," Elias confessed, voice barely above a whisper.

Caleb placed a firm hand on his shoulder. "Strength isn't the absence of fear. It's facing that fear and moving forward anyway. You've already shown more courage than most."

Elias swallowed hard, the words settling deep. He felt the weight of the war shift slightly, the burden lessening with shared understanding.

Their conversation was interrupted by a sudden commotion from the camp— a shout, sharp and urgent, slicing through the night's calm. Both men stood quickly, alert.

"Stay here," Caleb said, moving toward the noise.

Elias hesitated, then followed. They found Joseph rallying the men, his voice steady despite the tension. "Enemy scouts spotted near the northern ridge. Prepare yourselves."

The camp exploded into activity. Men grabbed muskets, loaded powder, and readied their positions. The quiet night transformed into a flurry of controlled chaos.

Elias's heart pounded as he moved to join his comrades. The familiar rhythm of battle returned, sharp and consuming.

From the ridge, faint shadows flickered—figures moving stealthily among the trees. The enemy was close.

Shots rang out, echoing through the mountain air. The men responded with disciplined volleys, muskets flashing in the darkness. The battle was swift, brutal, a clash of wills beneath the stars.

Elias fought fiercely, his every move fueled by the memories that haunted him and the hopes that sustained him. The adrenaline blurred pain and fear, replacing them with a fierce clarity.

When the last enemy scout fled into the night, the camp held its breath. No lives were lost, but the warning was clear—the enemy was closing in, more determined than ever.

As dawn approached, the men gathered to assess their strength and plan the next move. Exhaustion hung heavy, but the spirit remained unbroken.

Elias caught Caleb's eye and nodded—a silent promise that whatever came next, they would face it together.

Morning light spilled over the rugged ridge, painting the world in soft gold and shadow. The camp stirred with cautious energy, the fresh air carrying the scent of pine and earth, mingled with the faint acrid trace of last night's gunfire. The men moved methodically, checking weapons, tending to minor wounds, and preparing for the inevitable next step in their perilous journey.

Elias stood near the center of the camp, watching Joseph confer with the other officers. The weight of command sat heavily on Joseph's broad shoulders, his usual calm now tinged with the urgency of their situation. Elias felt a swell of respect—and a renewed determination to do whatever was needed.

Caleb approached, his face set with a grim resolve. "The scouts confirmed it," he said quietly. "The British are not just probing—they're gathering for a full assault. It won't be long before they come in force."

Joseph turned to Elias, his eyes meeting the younger man's with a steady fire. "We need every able hand ready. Today, we hold the line. Tomorrow, who knows what the gods will bring."

The men listened in silence, each wrestling with their own fears and hopes. Elias felt a chill, despite the warming sun. This was the crucible—where courage met fate.

Later, Elias found a quiet moment to speak with Caleb beneath a sprawling oak. The scout's eyes were sharp but weary.

"Do you think we can win?" Elias asked, voice low.

Caleb sighed. "We have to believe that we can. If we don't, then all this sacrifice means nothing."

Elias's gaze drifted to the distant horizon, where dark clouds gathered like a silent storm. "Sometimes I wonder what comes after all this. If we survive, what will be left of us?"

Caleb smiled faintly. "That's the question every soldier asks. We fight so the next generation won't have to."

The camp grew louder as preparations intensified. Fires were stoked, meals quickly eaten, and muskets cleaned and reloaded. Children of the militia—young boys and men barely past their youth—moved alongside hardened veterans, all bound by a common cause.

Elias spotted Martha across the camp, her determined face breaking through the tension like a beacon. She carried water and bandages, tending tirelessly to those in need. Their eyes met, and for a moment, the chaos faded. She nodded once—a silent encouragement that steadied his heart.

As the afternoon sun climbed higher, the sound of drums echoed faintly through the forest. The enemy was on the move.

Joseph gathered the men, his voice firm. "Form ranks. Hold steady. We fight not just for ourselves but for freedom, for family, for home."

The line advanced, muskets raised, eyes sharp. Elias stood shoulder to shoulder with Caleb and Joseph, feeling the steady rhythm of their breath and heartbeat as a singular force.

The first volley shattered the tense silence, a thunderous roar that rolled across the valley. Smoke curled in thick clouds, mingling with the scent of gunpowder and sweat.

Elias fired, reloaded, and fired again, his movements mechanical but precise. Around him, men shouted, cried, and fought with desperate resolve.

Time fractured into moments—each one stretched thin with fear and fierce hope. Elias caught glimpses of comrades falling, the flash of saber blades, the crash of bodies.

Suddenly, a cry rang out. Caleb was down, clutching his side, blood dark against his leather coat. Elias lunged forward, heart pounding, dragging him behind the cover of a fallen tree.

"Hold on, Caleb!" Elias urged, pressing a cloth to the wound. "You'll make it."

Caleb's eyes fluttered open, pain etched deep but his spirit unbroken. "Keep fighting... don't let them break the line."

Elias nodded fiercely, his resolve hardening. He helped Caleb to a safer spot, then returned to the fray with renewed fury.

The battle raged until the sun began to dip low, casting long shadows over the shattered landscape. When the guns finally fell silent, the camp was a tangle of exhaustion and quiet grief.

Joseph moved through the men, offering what comfort he could. Elias found Martha tending Caleb, whose breathing was shallow but steady.

In the fading light, Elias knelt beside Caleb. "You're going to live," he promised, though the words felt fragile.

Caleb managed a faint smile. "Because of you."

Elias's chest tightened. The war was far from over, but in this moment, amid the ruins and quiet, he felt something like hope—a fragile, flickering flame.

As night reclaimed the sky, Elias stared upward, whispering a prayer for those they'd lost and those still standing. The fight was not yet finished, but neither was their will to endure.

The night wrapped around the camp like a heavy cloak, thick with the scent of smoke and earth, the stars overhead pale against the darkened sky. Tension hung in the air, taut as a drawn bow, every shadow seeming to whisper warnings of the days to come. The men moved cautiously, their faces etched with exhaustion and determination, each step measured as if the ground itself might betray them.

Elias sat by a dwindling fire, the embers glowing weakly, casting flickering light over the dirt-streaked faces of those who remained awake. His hands trembled slightly as he carefully cleaned his musket, every movement methodical but his mind a whirlwind of memories and doubts. The ache in his side where a stray bullet had grazed him earlier throbbed steadily, a reminder of how close death had come—and how thin the line was between survival and sacrifice.

Martha approached quietly, a water skin in one hand, her eyes reflecting the firelight and something deeper—resolve mixed with sorrow. She sat beside him without a word, offering the water with a steady hand.

"Thank you," Elias murmured, accepting the gift. Their fingers brushed briefly, a small spark in the cold night.

Martha's gaze drifted toward the tents where the wounded lay, groans and whispered prayers mingling with the crackle of dying fires. "We've lost good men today," she said softly. "But we've held the line."

Elias nodded, swallowing the lump in his throat. "It feels like we're holding onto scraps sometimes. Like the ground beneath us is shifting, and we're just trying not to fall."

She smiled faintly, eyes steady. "That's why we fight—not just to hold, but to build. To stand firm, even when everything shakes."

Their conversation was interrupted by footsteps—Joseph, moving with a cautious but purposeful stride. His face was grim, the weight of leadership etched into every line.

"We've received word," Joseph said, lowering his voice. "The British are regrouping, planning a larger push within the week. We'll need to be ready."

Elias looked up, the firelight catching the determination in his eyes. "Then we rest tonight, gather strength. Tomorrow, we prepare."

Joseph nodded, a shadow of a smile crossing his face. "Aye. We fight not just with muskets, but with every ounce of heart we've got."

As Joseph moved on, Elias and Martha shared a look—a silent vow to stand together through the trials ahead.

Later, beneath a canopy of stars, Elias walked the perimeter of the camp. The night was alive with whispered fears and quiet courage, men standing guard, eyes sharp despite the exhaustion. He paused, listening to the soft murmur of voices and the occasional laugh—a fragile thread of normalcy in the midst of chaos.

His thoughts turned to Samuel, to the home he had left behind. Would that world still be waiting when this was over? Or was the price of freedom too high?

A sudden movement caught his eye—a figure stepping from the shadows. Caleb, leaning heavily on a staff, his wound still raw but his spirit unbroken.

"Thought I'd find you here," Caleb said, voice rough but steady.

Elias smiled, moving to steady his friend. "You're stronger than you look."

Caleb chuckled. "Had to be. Can't have you carrying all the weight."

They walked together, the silence between them comfortable. The firelight from the camp behind them seemed a distant memory, replaced by the stillness of the wild.

"Do you ever think about what comes after?" Elias asked, voice low.

Caleb's eyes reflected the stars. "All the time. But for now, we fight for today. For the chance to see that future."

Elias nodded, feeling the truth of those words settle deep within him.

As dawn approached, the camp began to stir once more, the cycle of preparation and battle unending. Yet in that quiet moment, beneath the vast sky, there was a flicker of hope—a promise that no matter the darkness, the light would return.

Chapter 9

A thin light crept slowly across the horizon, pale and hesitant as it spilled through the thick canopy of trees that sheltered the weary camp. A heavy silence hung in the cool morning air, broken only by the occasional soft rustle of leaves and the faint groans of those stirring from a restless night. Elias lay still for a long moment, feeling the stiffness in his limbs and the dull throb of the wound across his ribs—a stubborn reminder that the fight was far from over.

Around him, the camp stirred slowly, shadows moving like ghosts beneath ragged tents and crude lean-tos. Men sat hunched over fires long reduced to embers, some washing bloodied hands, others clutching makeshift bandages with trembling fingers. The air was thick with the scent of smoke and sweat, mingled with the faint, bitter tang of fear and loss.

Elias rose carefully, every movement a quiet ache, and walked toward the center of camp. His eyes, still sharp despite fatigue, scanned the faces of his comrades—faces etched with exhaustion, grief, and the stubborn flicker of determination that refused to die. Some sat in silence, their gazes lost in memories of battle; others exchanged low whispers, voices cracked with weariness. A few wept quietly, shoulders trembling under the weight of sorrow.

Near the fire, Martha moved with practiced grace, ladling out a thin stew from a battered pot. The simplicity of her actions, so ordinary in any other time, struck Elias with the contrast of their present reality. She caught his gaze and offered a small, tired smile—one that spoke volumes without a single word. Elias accepted the cup she handed him, the warmth a brief comfort against the chill settling into his bones.

His attention shifted beyond the fire, toward a somber patch of earth where freshly dug graves marked the cost of the previous day's fighting. Blankets and rough crosses stood silent witness to those who would not rise again, their absence felt keenly in the spaces they left behind. Elias's throat tightened as he spotted familiar features—faces of friends, neighbors, men who had fought and fallen alongside him.

He moved closer, his steps slow and reverent. Among the graves, an older man knelt, carefully patting down earth over a freshly made mound. Elias recognized him as Thomas, Samuel's old friend, a man who had once regaled the camp with stories of peaceful days and the promise of a better future. Now, his face was creased with grief so deep it seemed almost physical, as if sorrow weighed on his shoulders like a tangible burden.

"May they find peace," Thomas whispered, his voice breaking through the stillness. His hands trembled as they smoothed the soil, eyes fixed on the earth as though willing the dead to rest easy. "And may we find strength to carry on."

Elias approached cautiously, feeling the rawness of the moment. "We will," he said quietly, meeting Thomas's gaze. "We have to."

Thomas's eyes met his, filled with a mixture of pain and something resembling hope. "It's hard to believe sometimes. All this sacrifice... for what?"

The question hung heavy between them, as if the very air carried the weight of doubt and the bitter taste of loss. Elias searched his heart, looking for an answer that could make sense of the blood and tears.

"We fight for freedom," he said at last, his voice steady despite the turmoil beneath. "For the chance to live on our own terms, to build a life where our children won't have to hide in the woods or fight for every breath."

Thomas nodded slowly, swallowing hard. "Then we owe it to them—not just to fight, but to remember why."

The camp grew busier as the sun rose higher, the urgency of survival pushing aside some of the grief. Men tended to wounds with the scant supplies they had, wiping sweat and dirt from battered faces. Others repaired gear or gathered firewood, preparing for whatever trials lay ahead. The faces of the living were marked with both weariness and resolve—a fragile but persistent flame flickering against the gathering shadows of war.

Elias stood near the graves for a long moment longer, feeling the weight of the loss pressing down like a stone on his chest. Yet beneath that heavy burden, a small ember glowed—a fragile light of hope and determination that refused to be snuffed out, no matter how dark the night.

He turned away, feeling the pull of duty and the uncertain road ahead. As he walked back toward the bustle of the camp, Elias carried with him the faces of those lost, their memory a quiet strength in the face of a long and uncertain fight.

The camp's somber morning slowly transformed into restless activity as the pale light grew stronger, pushing back the shadows beneath the towering trees. A thin veil of mist hovered low to the ground, curling around the scattered tents and the smoldering embers of last night's fires. Men shuffled about with quiet purpose, their faces pale and drawn but eyes sharp with a simmering determination.

Joseph stood at the center of the clearing, his tall frame casting a long shadow on the packed earth. His coat, once proud and crisp, was now worn and stained, matching the weary look etched deep into his rugged features. Around him, a circle of men—some young, some old—formed a tense audience. They were comrades bound not only by their cause, but by the bitter reality of blood spilled and friends lost.

Joseph's voice cut through the cold morning air, steady but heavy. "Yesterday, we lost good men. Brothers who gave everything for the promise of freedom. Their sacrifice won't be forgotten—not by me, not by this group. But now, we stand at a crossroads. What do we do next?"

A thick silence followed. The men exchanged glances—some filled with anger, others with doubt. Elias stood among them, feeling the weight of the moment settle like a stone in his gut. The question was simple, but the answer was anything but. Every choice carried risk. Every path led through danger.

Garrett, a broad-shouldered man with a beard streaked by gray, spoke first, his voice rough from disuse and tiredness. "We're beat down, barely able to stand, much less fight. Maybe it's smarter to fall back—pull our wounded out, regroup, get our strength back. Charging headlong into another fight with what's left of us... it's a sure way to get more dead."

Some men nodded, relief softening their faces. The thought of retreat was tempting, a chance to catch their breath before the next storm.

Caleb, lean and deliberate, shook his head. "If we retreat, the enemy will follow. They'll take the ground, and we'll lose more than just this fight—we'll lose the heart of our cause. We can't give up the ground, not now."

Joseph listened carefully, weighing each voice. The burden of leadership was a constant companion, a heavy chain around his shoulders. His eyes flicked across the faces before him—young men like Elias, eyes bright with fear and hope; veterans hardened by years of struggle, their souls frayed but unbroken.

He took a deep breath. "I won't lie to you. The choice is hard. The risk is high. But we fight for more than land or glory. We fight for our homes, for our families, for the freedom to live as we choose. To honor those who fell yesterday, we must press on—carefully, yes, but with all the strength we can muster."

A murmur of assent grew louder, a fragile but growing fire of resolve. Elias felt his heart beat faster, the embers of courage kindling beneath the fatigue and fear.

As the meeting ended, the men dispersed into the camp, each lost in his own thoughts. Elias lingered near Joseph, whose face bore the unmistakable strain of a man carrying the weight of countless lives.

"Do you truly believe we can win?" Elias asked quietly, almost afraid of the answer.

Joseph's gaze softened, but his eyes held a quiet steel. "I believe we have to. Even when hope feels distant, we fight because surrender is not an option. Giving up means losing everything we've worked for."

The young man nodded slowly, wrestling with the same doubt that haunted them all. Around them, the camp began to hum with preparation—men cleaning their weapons, patching torn clothing, sharpening blades. The air was thick with the smell of smoke, dirt, and sweat.

Martha appeared at Elias's side, her hands full of clean cloths and a small pouch of herbs. "You need to rest when you can," she said softly, her voice gentle but firm. "This fight will take everything we have."

Elias managed a tired smile. "Rest feels like a luxury we can't afford."

She gave a faint nod, worry flickering behind her eyes. "And yet, it's the one thing that might keep us alive."

As the sun climbed higher, the camp's mood shifted—grief and fear still lingered, but they were tempered by a fierce determination. Men who had moments ago seemed ready to crumble now stood taller, steeling themselves for what lay ahead.

Elias wandered through the camp, his gaze settling on small moments—the quiet tending of wounds by makeshift nurses, the whispered prayers of those too broken to speak aloud, the firm clasp of comrades' hands in shared resolve. Each gesture was a silent vow that they would endure, that they would not let the dead fall in vain.

Later, Joseph gathered a small group of men, Elias among them. Maps were spread on a rough wooden table, ink and charcoal marking lines and shaded areas. Joseph pointed out positions, choke points, and paths of retreat. His voice was steady, authoritative.

"We move at first light tomorrow," he said. "Our goal is to hit the enemy before they can regroup. Surprise will be our greatest weapon. We'll divide into two groups—one to flank, one to strike head-on."

The plan was risky. There was no denying it. But the camp needed hope, and Joseph's leadership offered that, fragile as it was.

Elias studied the map, imagining the terrain, the possible sounds of battle— the clash of steel, the cries of men, the thunder of musket fire. His fingers brushed a spot marked in the woods nearby, the place where their line would hold.

"Will we lose more men?" he asked.

Joseph's jaw tightened. "Maybe. But we must believe each life lost brings us closer to the freedom we seek."

That night, as campfires burned low and the men settled for what little rest they could find, Elias lay awake beneath the stars. The weight of the day's decisions pressed on him, tangled with the memory of fallen friends and the fierce hope that still flickered deep inside.

In the quiet darkness, he made a promise—to himself, to those who would never see another dawn—to fight with every breath, for the cause, for the future.

The first light of dawn crept slowly over the horizon, casting a soft, golden glow across the camp. The world seemed to hold its breath, wrapped in a fragile silence that only moments before battle could bring. Elias stirred beneath his coarse blanket, muscles aching and mind restless. Sleep had been scarce; dreams haunted by yesterday's losses mingled with the hard reality waiting just beyond the trees.

Outside, the camp was already stirring. Men moved with a quiet urgency, speaking in hushed tones, their faces marked by both exhaustion and resolve. The smoke from the fading campfires drifted lazily upward, mingling with the early morning mist that clung to the underbrush.

Joseph was already awake, standing near the largest fire, staring into the embers as if seeking answers from the flames themselves. Elias approached, careful not to startle him.

"Morning, Joseph," Elias said softly.

Joseph turned, his tired eyes meeting Elias's. "Morning. Restless night?"

Elias nodded. "The same. I keep thinking about what's ahead."

Joseph gave a brief smile, weathered but kind. "That's the weight we all carry. But it sharpens the mind and steels the heart."

The camp began to prepare for the march. Horses were saddled, weapons checked and loaded, and last-minute instructions passed quietly from officer to soldier. The crackle of kindling and the soft murmur of prayers filled the air, weaving a tapestry of sounds that underscored the gravity of the moment.

Elias found himself beside Caleb, who was methodically cleaning his rifle.

The younger man's hands were steady despite the tension that gripped his features.

"How do you do it?" Elias asked. "Keep so calm?"

Caleb looked up briefly, meeting Elias's gaze. "I don't think about the fight itself. I think about what comes after. The freedom we're working for. That's what keeps me steady."

Elias nodded, feeling a flicker of comfort in those words. Hope, fragile and precious, was the only thing that could carry them through the dark days.

As the sun climbed higher, Joseph gathered the men once more. His voice rang clear and firm, echoing through the clearing.

"Today, we move to change the course of this fight. Remember, we are not just fighting soldiers—we're fighting for a future. For our families, for our homes. Stay sharp, watch each other's backs, and fight with honor."

The men responded with a unified shout, a roar of defiance that broke through the morning stillness. Elias felt his heart surge with a fierce pride, even as his hands trembled slightly with nervous energy.

The march began slowly, the ground damp beneath their boots and hooves. Trees whispered overhead as they passed, nature itself seeming to hold its breath in anticipation. The men moved with purpose, each step taking them closer to an uncertain fate.

Elias found himself walking beside Martha, whose quiet strength was a balm against the turmoil inside him.

"Are you ready?" she asked softly.

He glanced at her, seeing the determination in her eyes despite the worry that lurked beneath. "I don't know if anyone can ever truly be ready for what's coming."

She smiled faintly. "That's what makes us brave. Facing the unknown anyway."

They walked in silence for a time, the sounds of the forest surrounding them. Birds chirped tentatively, and a gentle breeze stirred the leaves, as if urging the soldiers forward.

Suddenly, Joseph signaled for a halt. The group fell silent, every sense alert. Ahead, through a break in the trees, they caught the first glimpse of the enemy's encampment—a sprawling cluster of tents and wagons, men moving about with careless confidence, unaware of the approaching storm.

Joseph gathered his officers quickly, whispering orders and plans with practiced urgency. Elias felt a thrill of adrenaline mix with a knot of fear deep in his stomach.

The attack would come swiftly, with the hope of catching the enemy off guard. The flankers would move silently through the woods, while the main force launched a direct strike.

Elias gripped his rifle tightly, breath shallow. He thought of his brother Samuel, gone too soon, and the faces of the friends lost yesterday. Their memories burned fiercely within him, fueling a courage he barely recognized in himself.

As the sun reached its peak, the men moved into position. The quiet before the storm was heavy and oppressive, broken only by the occasional rustle of leaves and the soft footsteps of the advancing soldiers.

Then, suddenly, the silence shattered.

Gunfire erupted like thunder, sharp and relentless. Shouts filled the air, mingling with the crack of muskets and the clash of steel. The battle had begun.

Elias dove behind a fallen log, heart pounding in his ears. Around him, men fell and rose, fought and screamed, the chaos a blur of smoke, blood, and desperation.

He fired his rifle again and again, feeling the recoil as a grim satisfaction. Each shot was a statement—a refusal to back down, a vow to keep fighting no matter the cost.

The enemy fought fiercely, their lines wavering but not breaking. Elias caught sight of Joseph at the front, rallying the men with fierce determination, his voice carrying over the din of battle.

The woods echoed with the sounds of war—shouts, gunfire, the thud of bodies hitting the ground. Elias's breath came fast, muscles burning with exertion.

Suddenly, a sharp cry rang out beside him. Turning, he saw Caleb clutching his side, blood seeping through his fingers.

"Hold the line!" Caleb gasped. Elias rushed to support him, helping the wounded man behind cover.

Amid the chaos, Elias realized this was more than a fight for territory. It was a test of their very souls, a crucible forging their courage and resolve.

The sun began to dip toward the horizon, casting long shadows over the battlefield. Exhaustion gnawed at Elias, but the fire inside him refused to dim.

As the enemy began to retreat, the men of the camp let out a weary cheer. They had held the line—for now.

Elias looked around at the fallen, the battered faces of his comrades, and knew the cost was far from over. But today, they had taken a stand. They had shown what it meant to fight for freedom.

And in that moment, amidst the smoke and silence, Elias felt something stir—a fragile, fierce hope that maybe, just maybe, they could win.

Dusk settled like a soft blanket over the battered battlefield. Fierce din of combat had finally faded into a tense quiet, punctuated only by distant groans and the crackling of dying fires. Elias stood among his weary comrades, the weight of the day pressing down on his shoulders as heavily as his bloodstained coat.

Around him, men moved slowly, faces etched with exhaustion and grief. Some knelt beside the fallen, whispering prayers or offering comfort, others scanned the horizon, eyes wary for any sign of a renewed attack. Air hung thick with the scent of smoke, sweat, and earth disturbed by so many boots and horses.

Elias's gaze drifted toward the woods beyond the clearing, where shadows stretched long and ominous. Once a refuge, the forest now seemed a place of silent judgment—holding its secrets close.

Joseph approached, his face grim but resolute. "We've held the field today," he said quietly, "but the fight isn't over. Enemy will regroup, and we must be ready."

Elias nodded, though the ache in his chest told a different story. Price of victory etched in every fallen brother, every whispered farewell, every empty space at the campfire.

Work began—the grim task of tending to wounded and burying the dead. Elias labored alongside others, his hands steady despite the turmoil within. Each grave stood as a silent testament to sacrifice, a reminder that freedom came at a cost no man could fully pay.

As night deepened, camp grew quieter. Men gathered around smoldering fires, sharing what little food remained and exchanging stories that felt too fragile against darkness. Elias found himself near the fire's edge, staring into flames as memories crowded his mind.

Thoughts turned to Samuel—the brother who had taught him to wield a hammer and dream of a better world. The thought was both painful and comforting, a tether to a past that fueled his resolve.

Martha sat beside him, eyes reflecting flickering light. "You carry him with you," she said softly. "In every step you take."

Elias smiled faintly, grateful for her presence. "I hope I'm worthy of that."

Sudden movement drew his attention. Joseph spoke with Caleb, whose wounds had been dressed but still left him pale and weak. Voices were low, urgent.

"We'll need scouts at first light," Joseph said. "We can't afford to be caught unprepared."

Caleb nodded, grim determination flickering in his tired eyes. "I'll do what I can."

Elias felt a swell of admiration for the younger man's courage. Despite pain, Caleb was ready to face whatever came next.

Later, as camp settled into uneasy rest, Elias took a solitary walk toward the edge of the woods. Night was cool and still, stars overhead shining like distant beacons. He paused beneath an ancient oak, its gnarled branches reaching skyward as if in silent prayer.

Here, away from murmurs and shadows of camp, Elias allowed himself a moment to breathe—to feel weight of the day and flicker of hope that remained.

Thoughts turned to men he fought beside, dreams they carried like fragile flames against darkness. Ordinary men, with fears and doubts, yet in this moment, something more. Bearers of a cause greater than themselves.

Future remained uncertain, road ahead perilous. But as Elias looked to stars, quiet certainty settled in his heart: they would fight on. For freedom, for justice, for promise of a new dawn.

Returning to camp, Elias resolved to rest what little he could. Tomorrow would bring new challenges, new dangers, and new hopes.

But tonight, beneath vast sky, he let himself believe that even in darkest times, light could still shine through.

A chill wind swept through the camp just before dawn, carrying the sharp scent of damp earth and smoke. The men stirred slowly from uneasy sleep, their bodies aching but minds alert. Elias rose from his blanket, pulling his coat tight against the cold. Around him, flickering lanterns and smoldering embers cast long shadows across the faces of soldiers preparing for another uncertain day.

The morning air buzzed with a quiet urgency. Joseph's voice cut through the dim light, calling the men to gather near the clearing. Soldiers assembled quickly, their tired eyes scanning the trees, searching for signs of the enemy. Caleb stood among them, leaning heavily on a makeshift crutch, determination still burning bright despite his injury.

"We'll send out scouts to the north and east," Joseph announced, his tone steady but serious. "We need to know if they're moving, how many, and where."

Elias volunteered without hesitation. "I'll go," he said, stepping forward.

Joseph looked at him with a mixture of pride and concern. "Be careful. We can't afford to lose you now."

As the scouting party set off into the misty woods, Elias's heart pounded with a mixture of fear and resolve. Branches brushed against his face, and the soft crunch of leaves beneath his boots became the only sound in the stillness. Every shadow seemed to shift with hidden threats, every whisper of wind a warning.

Minutes stretched like hours as they moved deeper into the forest. Suddenly, a rustle ahead froze them in place. Elias signaled for silence, raising his hand. Through the thick brush, they spotted figures—enemy soldiers, moving cautiously but with purpose.

Elias's pulse quickened. He crouched low, watching as the enemy paused near a fallen log, exchanging hurried words. The scouts counted their numbers silently, committing every detail to memory.

When the patrol retreated, Elias led the way back to camp, breath coming in sharp bursts. Upon arrival, Joseph listened intently as Elias and the others relayed what they'd seen: the enemy was regrouping, preparing for another assault, and their numbers were larger than anticipated.

Plans shifted quickly. Trenches were deepened, sentries doubled, and weapons cleaned and readied. The men moved with grim efficiency, knowing that the battle for survival was far from over.

Later, as Elias took a moment to catch his breath beside the fire, Martha approached, carrying a small bundle of bread and cheese. She handed it to him with a weary smile. "You look like you could use this."

Gratefully, Elias accepted the food. "Thank you, Martha. You always seem to know when I need it most."

She shrugged lightly, eyes softening. "We all lean on each other out here."

Their brief exchange was interrupted by a sudden shout from the perimeter. Joseph sprinted past, calling orders. Elias rose instantly, heart hammering— another wave was coming.

Men scrambled to their positions, faces set with determination and fear. The air grew electric with anticipation as enemy forces emerged from the trees, their war cries cutting through the morning stillness.

Shots rang out, muskets blazing as the battle erupted anew. Elias gripped his rifle tightly, aiming carefully, each pull of the trigger a mixture of survival and desperation. Around him, comrades fought fiercely, voices rising and falling in the chaotic symphony of war.

Smoke curled thickly, mingling with the cries of the wounded and the clash of steel. Time seemed to blur as moments stretched into eternity, the fight raging with relentless fury.

Amidst the chaos, Elias caught glimpses of Joseph rallying the men, his voice a beacon of strength. Martha moved swiftly, tending to the injured, her hands steady despite the turmoil.

Pain and loss surrounded them, yet so did courage and hope.

As the sun climbed higher, the enemy began to falter, their lines breaking under the relentless defense. Cheers rose from the defenders, exhaustion mingling with triumph.

When silence finally fell, it was heavy and profound. Men stood among the fallen, breathing hard, eyes haunted but resolute.

Elias sank to the ground, limbs trembling. He looked around at the faces of those who had fought beside him—scarred, weary, but alive.

Martha knelt beside him, her touch gentle. "You did well," she said softly.

He met her gaze, finding in her eyes a flicker of promise—a belief that, despite the darkness, dawn was still possible.

Together, they faced what lay ahead, bound by the unyielding hope that freedom was worth every sacrifice.

Chapter 10

Shadows stretched and trembled across the morning floor as light sifted through the tangled branches. Smoke lingered like a stubborn ghost, weaving through the trees and curling upward toward the grey sky. Silence, heavy and uneasy, settled over the camp as men stirred from restless slumber, shadows of yesterday's battle still etched on their faces.

Elias remained seated on a fallen log, fingers absently tracing the rough bark as his mind replayed the chaos of the day before. Each breath drew in the acrid scent of gunpowder and damp earth, mixing with the metallic taste of fear that still clung to his throat. Around him, scattered remnants of the fight told silent stories — a discarded musket leaning against a tree, bloodied cloth pinned beneath a rock, footprints pressed deep in the mud.

Nearby, a pair of worn boots caught his eye, caked in mud and carelessly abandoned. For a heartbeat, he imagined the soldier who'd worn them — young, hopeful, full of dreams now extinguished. A weight settled on his chest, heavier than any wound.

A gentle voice broke through his reverie. "Elias." Joseph approached, his weary eyes searching his friend's face. "There's much to discuss. The men need direction."

Slowly rising, Elias swallowed past the lump in his throat and followed Joseph toward the officers' circle. The faces gathered there bore the same mixture of fatigue and determination — men grasping for purpose in the aftermath of loss.

Joseph's voice rang clear. "We cannot afford to linger in sorrow. Our enemy is regrouping, and reinforcements will come soon."

Murmurs spread as the officers exchanged tense glances. Captain Hawkins, known for his blunt pragmatism, stepped forward. "If we wait, they will crush us beneath their numbers."

"Retreat could save lives, but it may also crush morale," another officer argued, eyes darting around the circle.

Elias found himself caught between urgency and caution. Every decision carried a heavy price. He glanced at the young faces around him, some barely men, their eyes wide with fear and exhaustion. "We need a way to fight smart, not just hard," he said quietly. "A strike behind enemy lines could slow their reinforcements."

Joseph nodded slowly. "That's a risk, but one we might have to take."

Suddenly, Martha appeared, carrying a satchel heavy with bandages and supplies. She moved among the wounded, offering quiet comfort, her touch gentle but sure. When her eyes met Elias's, a flicker of warmth passed between them — a brief reprieve from the storm around them. She gave a small nod, silently acknowledging the shared burden.

Hours slipped by as plans formed and shifted. Elias felt the weight of every decision pressing down. Finally, the group agreed: a small force would slip behind enemy lines, sabotage supply routes, and delay reinforcements long enough for the main camp to prepare defenses.

Without hesitation, Elias stepped forward. "I'll go," he said, voice steady despite the churn of fear beneath his skin. "I know these woods. I can find the safest path."

Joseph's hand landed on his shoulder, firm and reassuring. "Your courage keeps us going. We'll trust you with this."

Preparations began under the cloak of twilight. Elias checked his rifle, packed the few belongings he deemed essential, and said quiet goodbyes to comrades who shared his resolve. Each step was heavy, but determination burned brighter with every breath.

Night deepened and the camp settled into uneasy quiet. Flames flickered low in the fire pits, casting dancing shadows on faces marked by grief and hope. Elias sat near the fire, staring into the flames, memories of fallen friends swirling like smoke.

Laughter from long ago, promises whispered under stars, the weight of loss—each mingled in his mind. He reached into his pocket and fingered a small, worn carving of a tree his brother had given him long ago. It felt like a talisman, grounding him amid the uncertainty.

Suddenly, footsteps approached. Martha's voice broke the silence. "Elias, I brought you something." She handed him a small bundle of dried meat and bread. "You'll need your strength."

He smiled faintly. "Thank you. It means more than you know."

They spoke quietly then, sharing stories of home and hope, drawing strength from each other. The night stretched on, filled with unspoken fears and quiet courage.

Before long, Joseph called him aside. "Rest when you can. Tomorrow will test every ounce of your strength."

Elias nodded, settling against a tree as the fire's warmth faded into cool night air. Stars stretched overhead—silent witnesses to the battle yet to come.

Inside, a fierce resolve blazed. The road ahead promised danger, but freedom demanded sacrifice. And Elias was ready to pay the price.

Dawn barely touched the sky when Elias stirred from a restless sleep. His body ached from the tension of anticipation and the cold night that had seeped into his bones. Around him, campfires sputtered low embers and the quiet murmurs of men preparing for what lay ahead filled the air. Every rustle of canvas, every whispered instruction, sharpened the edge of the coming hours.

He rose silently, careful not to disturb Martha, who still slept wrapped in her blanket nearby. The weight of the rifle in his hands grounded him as he moved toward the gathering of soldiers assembling at the edge of the camp. Faces were grim, eyes hard with determination and shadowed by fatigue.

Joseph met him there, his expression grave but steady. "We move soon. The fewer we are, the less chance of being spotted. We strike quick, and we vanish."

Elias nodded, swallowing the knot of anxiety tightening in his chest. The forest awaited, dense and unforgiving, yet familiar from years of wandering its paths as a boy. He knew every twist and hollow — knowledge that could mean the difference between life and death.

Captain Hawkins stood before the men, his voice low and commanding. "This mission is dangerous. Supplies we destroy will cripple the enemy's ability to fight. Without them, their reinforcements will falter. Remember, silence is our ally. No unnecessary noise. No leaving anyone behind."

A murmur of assent passed through the group. Elias's gaze drifted to the young men around him—some barely more than boys, clutching rifles with trembling hands, others hardened by battle but visibly strained by the weight of what they must do. He felt the fierce need to protect them, even as he understood the harsh reality: not all would return.

A brief prayer whispered through the cool morning air. Martha stood at the edge of camp, her eyes steady despite the fear that flickered behind them. Their eyes met for a moment, an unspoken promise passing between them. Elias drew strength from that fleeting connection, a tether to home and hope.

The strike force moved out, stepping cautiously beneath the canopy of ancient trees. The forest welcomed them with muffled sounds — the crunch of leaves underfoot, the distant call of a bird startled by their passage. Every shadow seemed alive, every rustle a potential threat. Elias led, senses alert to every detail, every shift in the wind.

As they navigated the narrow trail, whispers of conversation floated through the group — stories of families waiting behind, dreams deferred by war, and quiet hopes for a day when the fighting would cease. Despite the tension, camaraderie forged a fragile bond.

Suddenly, a twig snapped sharply ahead. Hearts hammered. Elias signaled a halt, fingers curling tightly around the rifle. Every man froze, breath caught in silent anticipation. Eyes scanned the underbrush. Nothing moved.

After a tense moment, Joseph whispered, "False alarm. Move on."

Relief mingled with renewed caution as they pressed forward, each step deliberate and careful. The supply depot lay several miles deeper in the forest, guarded but vulnerable if struck swiftly.

Approaching the clearing, Elias crouched low, peering through the thicket. Lanterns flickered faintly, illuminating stacks of barrels and crates — gunpowder, food, munitions vital to the enemy's war effort. Around the perimeter, sentries paced with weary eyes.

Captain Hawkins motioned to split the group into two teams: one to create a diversion, the other to ignite the caches. Elias volunteered for the latter, feeling the weight of responsibility settle firmly.

Under cover of darkness and whispers, the team moved in, hearts pounding like war drums. Elias's hands trembled slightly but did not falter as he doused the barrels in oil, careful not to make a sound.

A sudden cough from behind made him freeze — Private Lawson's face pale with terror. Elias's eyes locked with the younger man's, a silent command to stay still.

Minutes stretched unbearably before the signal came. A flare shot skyward from the diversion team, followed by the crackle of gunfire and shouts that shattered the night's stillness.

Flames erupted in the depot, licking skyward with fierce hunger. Explosions rocked the clearing as munitions ignited, sending shockwaves through the forest. Elias dropped to the ground, ears ringing, heart racing.

"Retreat!" Joseph's voice cut through the chaos.

The team scattered into the trees, running on instinct and memory. Branches tore at faces, roots threatened to trip, but retreat was imperative.

Behind them, enemy voices shouted in confusion and anger. Elias's breath came in ragged gasps, lungs burning as he pushed deeper into the woods, every sense alert for pursuit.

Pain seared through his calf — a shallow cut from a hidden branch, but the sting fueled his adrenaline. He glanced back briefly; no pursuers close enough yet.

When the forest finally swallowed their footsteps, the group regrouped in a shadowed hollow, breaths heaving, faces streaked with soot and sweat.

Captain Hawkins exhaled sharply. "Mission accomplished. Supplies destroyed, enemy delayed."

Relief washed through Elias, tempered by exhaustion and the weight of what the next days might bring.

Joseph clapped him on the shoulder. "You did well, Elias. Couldn't have done it without you."

The men settled into wary silence, tending wounds and sharing whispered words of encouragement. Night fell fully, stars sparkling faintly above the canopy.

Elias sat apart, staring into the darkness. Thoughts tumbled — memories of home, the faces of fallen comrades, the fragile hope that freedom might come at last.

A soft voice broke the silence. Martha stepped into the clearing, her eyes bright but shadowed by fatigue. "You made it back."

He nodded, managing a tired smile. "We did what we came to do."

She knelt beside him, pressing a cool hand to his cheek. "And now, we wait."

Smoke still hung thick in the air, mingling with the damp scent of crushed leaves and pine needles. The forest had settled into an uneasy quiet, as if holding its breath after the explosion's fury. But inside Elias, the storm raged on, relentless and consuming.

The trek back to camp was slow and cautious. Each footfall was measured, the men moving through the shadows with a wary vigilance born of recent chaos. Elias's leg throbbed sharply with every step, the scratch from the branch more painful than he'd expected. Still, he refused to let it slow him— not now, not when so much depended on their success.

Martha walked beside him, a steady presence against the darkened backdrop. Her quiet strength buoyed him more than words ever could. Though exhaustion weighed heavy in her eyes, she pushed onward, sharing the burden without complaint.

"Did you hear?" whispered Tom, a lanky scout trailing just behind. "Word is, the enemy's already rallying troops. They won't forget tonight."

Elias nodded grimly. "They'll come, sooner than we hope. But we've bought time."

The weight of the mission settled deeper as they neared camp. Faces that had seemed resolute now flickered with doubt and fear. The cost of war was never clearer than in those moments—every victory shadowed by the toll it took on bodies and spirits alike.

Captain Hawkins was waiting, pacing near the flickering firelight. When Elias approached, the captain's eyes held a mixture of pride and sorrow.

"You held your ground well," Hawkins said quietly, clapping a hand to Elias's shoulder. "Not many would have."

Pain threatened to break through Elias's stoic facade, but he swallowed it down. "We did what needed doing. The supplies won't feed their war machine."

"True," Hawkins agreed, his voice heavy with weariness. "But this fight isn't over. Not by a long shot."

The camp was a hive of activity—medics tending wounds, cooks preparing scant rations, men cleaning weapons with grim focus. Elias found himself drifting toward the group, drawn into the quiet conversations that tried to stitch together the frayed edges of morale.

"You alright?" Joseph's voice pulled him back. "That scratch looks worse than you're letting on."

Elias flexed his leg carefully. "Just a scratch. Nothing serious."

Joseph's brow furrowed. "You'll want to get it checked. Infection can set in fast out here."

Before Elias could respond, a sudden shout rang out from the other side of the camp. Heads turned sharply as soldiers hurried toward the noise. Elias's heart quickened.

A rider had arrived—dust-covered, breathless, eyes wide with urgency. As he dismounted, all gathered around, waiting for news.

"The enemy's moving," the rider gasped. "Larger forces than we expected. They're heading this way."

A hush fell over the camp. The night's fragile peace shattered like glass.

Captain Hawkins stepped forward, his face a mask of determination. "Prepare for battle. We hold our ground here. No retreat."

Elias's stomach twisted with a mixture of fear and resolve. The raid had been only the beginning. Now the real test was at hand.

In the following hours, the camp transformed into a fortress. Sharpened stakes were planted, trenches dug hastily. Men checked weapons and tightened grips, exchanging fierce glances that spoke louder than words.

Martha moved among them, her presence a balm in the tension. She carried bandages and water, offering quiet comfort where she could.

As dawn's first light bled through the trees, Elias sat beside the dying fire, eyes tracing the slow climb of the sun. He thought of home, of the family he might never see again. The dream of freedom felt distant, yet burning brighter than ever.

Joseph sat beside him, breaking the silence. "We fight for more than survival. For those who can't fight. For those who dream."

Elias nodded, gripping his rifle tighter. The war was far from over. But so long as breath filled his lungs and fire burned in his heart, he would stand and fight.

The camp buzzed with a tense energy as the morning sun climbed higher, casting long shadows across the sharpened stakes and hastily dug trenches. Every movement was deliberate, every whispered word laced with urgency. The men and women preparing for the looming battle knew what was at stake—not just their lives, but the fragile hopes of a fledgling cause.

Elias moved among the fighters, feeling the weight of responsibility settle heavier than ever before. Faces once bright with youthful confidence now bore the marks of sleepless nights and unspoken fears. Yet, beneath the surface, a fierce determination burned. This was no longer just a raid or skirmish—it was a fight for their very future.

Captain Hawkins stood atop a fallen log, his voice clear and commanding as he addressed the gathered fighters. "Today we face an enemy larger and stronger than before. But we have something they do not—heart, and the will to defend what is ours. Stand your ground, fight as one, and we will prevail."

A murmur of agreement rippled through the crowd. Elias found himself tightening his grip on his rifle, heart pounding in rhythm with the rising tension. He glanced toward Martha, who met his gaze with a steady nod, her eyes shining with quiet resolve.

Nearby, Joseph checked his musket one last time, then turned to Elias. "We've come this far, brother. Whatever happens next, know I'm with you."

Elias swallowed hard, nodding in return. "Always."

The air grew thick with anticipation as the first signs of movement appeared at the edge of the tree line. Figures emerged—shadows against the morning light, growing steadily larger and more defined. The enemy was advancing.

"Hold!" Captain Hawkins called, raising his sword. The fighters steadied themselves, muscles coiled like springs ready to unleash.

The clash came suddenly—gunfire cracking through the air, yells echoing like thunder. The forest erupted into chaos as men charged forward, meeting the enemy in a brutal contest of wills.

Elias found himself in the heart of the battle, every sense alive with adrenaline. Smoke stung his eyes, sweat dripped down his brow, and the thunder of footsteps and shouted orders filled his ears.

A soldier lunged toward him, musket raised. Elias dodged just in time, countering with a sharp strike that sent the man sprawling. Around him, comrades fought fiercely, each swing and shot a desperate bid for survival.

Amid the fury, Elias caught sight of Martha tending a wounded fighter nearby, her hands steady despite the blood and dust. For a brief moment, their eyes met—a silent promise to endure whatever came next.

Hours passed like a blur. The battle surged and ebbed, neither side willing to yield. Elias's leg throbbed sharply, a reminder of the earlier injury, but he pushed through the pain. Every breath, every heartbeat was a testament to his resolve.

At last, the enemy began to falter, their lines breaking under the relentless pressure. Cheers rose from the camp, mingled with cries of grief for those lost.

Captain Hawkins approached Elias, sweat and grime streaking his face. "You fought well, lad. We've held the line."

Elias nodded, exhaustion threatening to overwhelm him. Around them, survivors gathered, the weight of victory tempered by the cost.

As the sun dipped low, casting a golden glow over the battered camp, Elias allowed himself a moment to breathe—to feel the weight of what they'd endured and the hope that still flickered in the fading light.

Martha stepped beside him, her hand finding his. "This is just the beginning," she said softly. "But together, we'll see it through."

Elias squeezed her hand, determination settling deep within. The road ahead would be long and perilous, but with friends like these, he believed they could face whatever darkness came their way.

Dusk folded over the camp like a heavy blanket, cooling the air and softening the harsh scars left by the day's relentless fighting. Shadows stretched long across the ground, creeping between tents and makeshift shelters where men and women nursed wounds or sat in quiet reflection. The firelight flickered warmly against the faces around the campfire circles, illuminating exhaustion, grief, and a fragile, stubborn hope that refused to be extinguished.

Elias lowered himself onto a roughly hewn log near the dying embers of the campfire, every movement sending a sharp ache through the injured muscles of his leg. The dull throbbing reminded him that the price of the day was not yet fully paid. Around him, soft murmurs of conversation drifted through the night—the sharing of stories from the battle, whispered prayers for those who would not wake, and murmured plans for the days ahead.

Martha moved gracefully through the gathering, her presence a steadying force amid the restless energy of the camp. She carried a small bundle of herbs and cloth, handing out water, offering comfort, and quietly tending to the wounded. When she reached Elias, her eyes softened with a mix of worry and tenderness.

"You're pushing yourself too hard," she said softly as she knelt beside him, brushing damp strands of hair from his sweaty forehead. "You need to rest."

Elias shook his head, forcing a tired smile. "Rest can wait," he murmured. "There's too much at stake. If I stop, even for a moment, I'm letting everyone down."

Her fingers lingered on his cheek, warm and gentle. "You're not alone in this. You don't have to carry the weight by yourself."

Before Elias could reply, Joseph approached, his face drawn but determined. "Captain Hawkins has called a meeting," he announced quietly. "Says we need to plan for what comes next. The enemy isn't finished with us."

Elias nodded, grim determination settling over him like armor. He stood, brushing dust from his worn trousers. Martha rose with him, her hand briefly finding his—a silent reassurance that they faced the coming storm together.

The meeting was called at the largest tent, where a crude map was spread across a wooden table illuminated by the flicker of oil lamps. The faces around it were grim, voices low but urgent as strategy was laid out.

Captain Hawkins stood at the head of the table, his voice steady and commanding. "We've won a battle today, but the war is far from over. The enemy will regroup. Their numbers grow, and they will come back with more firepower and greater fury."

The group exchanged tense glances. Elias traced the rough lines on the map—forests, rivers, the hills that cradled their makeshift stronghold. He knew these woods better than anyone, and the thought of enemy soldiers pushing through them sent a shiver down his spine.

"We can't just hold our ground," Hawkins continued. "We need to strike first, strike fast, and strike smart. We must disrupt their supply lines, weaken their reinforcements, and sow confusion among their ranks."

A murmur of agreement ran through the group. Strategies were debated: small skirmishes to draw the enemy out, night raids to disrupt their camps, using the terrain to their advantage. Elias felt the weight of every decision pressing down on him.

As the discussion wore on, Martha's quiet voice cut through the tension. "And what of the civilians caught in this? The families in the nearby settlements? They're vulnerable."

Hawkins met her gaze with a nod. "Protecting them is a priority. We'll assign scouts and send messengers to warn the villages. No one fights alone in this."

Later, as the meeting broke up and the fighters returned to their tents and fires, Elias found himself drawn to the edge of the camp, where the forest loomed dark and silent. The stars stretched wide overhead, a glittering tapestry that seemed both endless and indifferent.

He sat beneath a towering oak, his breath steadying despite the exhaustion threatening to drag him under. Thoughts of home pressed in—memories of his mother's gentle hands, his father's steady voice, the quiet comfort of familiar rooms. That world seemed so far away now, yet it was what he fought to protect.

Martha's footsteps approached softly, and she settled beside him without a word. For a long moment, they simply shared the quiet, listening to the night's gentle whispers.

"You can't carry this all by yourself," she said at last, her voice barely above a whisper.

He met her gaze, raw and honest. "I don't want to. I never wanted to. But sometimes it feels like the burden is mine alone."

Her hand found his, warm and sure in the cool night. "You're not alone. We all carry it—each of us in our own way. Together, we're stronger than any army."

Elias drew a slow breath, feeling the truth in her words settle deep within. "Together," he agreed.

Their quiet moment was interrupted by a soft rustle nearby. Joseph emerged from the shadows, his expression unreadable. "Captain Hawkins wants us to patrol the eastern ridge at dawn," he said. "He thinks the enemy might try to flank us there."

Martha nodded. "We should prepare, then. Get what rest we can."

Elias stood, muscles stiff but resolve unbroken. The road ahead was uncertain and dangerous, but the strength of those beside him gave hope.

As the camp settled into uneasy rest, the crackling firelight casting dancing shadows across tired faces, Elias allowed himself a moment to look up at the stars again. Somewhere in that vast sky, a future waited—one they would fight tooth and nail to reach.

Chapter 11

Elias woke stiff and sore, the weight of the previous day's battles still pressing into his limbs. Outside, the hills were cloaked in cold, heavy clouds hanging low. Yet even in the chill and fatigue, there was no time to linger. The air buzzed with restless energy as fighters stirred, sharpening weapons, exchanging hushed plans, and stealing brief moments of quiet before the day's dangers unfurled.

He pulled his coat tighter, eyes scanning the camp. Faces bore the marks of sleepless nights and battles fought—not just wounds on skin but shadows deeper in their eyes. Yet beneath the weariness lay a steely determination, a shared commitment that bound them together stronger than any chain.

Captain Hawkins gathered the group near the eastern ridge, where the forest thinned and the land dropped sharply away. The captain's voice was calm but urgent as he spoke, outlining the day's orders.

"We know the enemy scouts have been seen near these hills," Hawkins said, pointing toward the tree line. "They're probing for weaknesses. We'll send a patrol to watch the ridge and delay any advance. If they try to flank us, we'll meet them here."

Elias felt the familiar surge of adrenaline as his name was called. "You and Joseph will take the western side. Martha and I will cover the east. Stay alert, and stay alive."

The patrol moved out swiftly, the crunch of boots on frost-hardened earth breaking the morning's stillness. The trees stood sentinel, their skeletal branches reaching skyward, stripped bare by winter's breath. The forest held its secrets tight — shadows that shifted, eyes that watched unseen.

As they settled into position along the ridge, Elias's thoughts turned inward. Memories flickered unbidden: his father's rough hands guiding him through blacksmith lessons, the laughter shared with his brother Samuel before the world grew dark and uncertain. That warmth seemed so distant now, a fragile ember amid the cold.

Martha's voice broke through the quiet. "You carry a heavy burden," she said softly, moving closer. "But you don't have to carry it alone."

He nodded, grateful for her steady presence. "I've learned that. The harder part is trusting others with that burden."

A sudden rustle in the underbrush snapped their attention outward. Fingers tightened on weapon handles. The forest seemed to hold its breath.

From the trees emerged a lone figure — a scout, weary but unharmed. He raised a hand in greeting, eyes sharp and alert.

"Enemy movement," the scout whispered urgently. "A small force is advancing through the valley below. They're scouting for a way to outflank us."

Elias exchanged a quick glance with Martha, then with Joseph, who was signaling from the western flank. The enemy's plan was clear.

"We'll hold here," Elias said firmly. "Buy time and force them into a disadvantage. Let Hawkins know."

The tension in the air tightened as the patrol prepared for the coming clash. The ridge was their line — the ground where futures would be decided.

The ridge seemed to hold its breath, the cold morning air thick with tension. Elias crouched low behind the moss-covered log, his breath coming out in visible puffs that quickly vanished into the gray dawn. Every sense was on high alert, every muscle taut, waiting for the inevitable storm to break.

Below them, in the shadowed valley, the enemy scouts moved like ghosts— quiet, precise, and deadly. Their uniforms were dark, blending seamlessly with the forest floor and twisted branches. Elias could see their bayonets gleaming faintly when they caught the weak sunlight.

Martha leaned closer, her dark eyes sharp and unwavering. "They'll try to take the high ground. If they do, we're finished."

Elias met her gaze, feeling the weight of command settle heavier than ever before. "We won't let that happen. Not while we breathe."

Joseph, stationed on the western flank, raised his hand in a subtle signal—an arrangement they had practiced countless times before. Elias and Martha exchanged a quick nod. The plan was simple: Joseph would launch a swift strike on the enemy's left flank to unsettle their formation, while Elias and Martha held the central ridge line, prepared to fall back only if overwhelmed.

Then the silence shattered.

The sharp crack of muskets echoed through the trees, followed by the whistling scream of arrows. Smoke curled into the cold air, twisting in ethereal tendrils before dissipating. Suddenly, the forest erupted into chaos.

Elias's heart pounded as he raised his musket, the cold metal familiar in his hands. He fired twice, breath steady despite the pounding noise all around. Nearby, Martha's rifle cracked sharply, each shot precise and deadly.

From the western edge, Joseph's small band emerged like a pack of wolves, arrows flying and bayonets flashing as they struck at the enemy's flank. Elias caught sight of Joseph grappling with a soldier twice his size—muscles straining, faces twisted in fierce determination. Elias moved forward, joining the melee.

Steel clanged against steel as Elias swung his musket butt, knocking the enemy soldier backward just enough to gain the upper hand. Joseph wasted no time, plunging his bayonet deep into the attacker's side. The enemy fell, lifeless, but the battle raged on.

Suddenly, Elias's voice cut through the din. "Flank! They're trying to encircle us!"

Martha's eyes widened. Without hesitation, she moved to intercept the approaching scouts. Her hands were steady, even as sweat mingled with the grime on her face. Each shot found its mark, dropping enemy soldiers who tried to sneak behind their lines.

The ridge became a blur of motion—soldiers shouting orders, muskets firing, the clash of steel. Elias ducked behind a tree just in time to avoid a flying blade. His heart hammered as he took aim at an enemy scout advancing through the underbrush.

A quick succession of shots rang out, and the scout fell, clutching his chest. Elias pressed forward, his muscles burning, his lungs gasping for air.

Amid the chaos, movement caught his eye—a young soldier stumbling through the thicket, blood staining his uniform. Without hesitation, Elias dashed toward him, musket raised.

Just as the young man faltered, an enemy soldier lunged from the shadows, blade aimed for his neck. Elias swung the butt of his musket with all his strength, the impact sending the attacker reeling.

"Can you stand?" Elias asked, gripping the soldier's arm.

The young man nodded weakly, wincing. "I think so."

Together, they moved back toward the safety of their lines, the sounds of battle echoing around them.

Reaching the camp, Elias lowered the young soldier gently. "We need a medic. Now."

One of the camp's healers hurried over, examining the wound with practiced hands. "It's deep, but not fatal. We'll manage."

Elias exhaled slowly, fatigue washing over him. The adrenaline that had kept him sharp moments ago now left a dull ache in his limbs.

Captain Hawkins approached, his face grim but proud. "Good work holding the ridge," he said. "But this is just the beginning. The enemy will come again—stronger, smarter. We must be ready."

Elias nodded, the weight of command settling even heavier. He glanced at the faces around him—friends, comrades, all worn but unbroken. In their eyes, he saw the same resolve that burned within himself.

Night began to fall, and the camp settled into uneasy silence. Fires flickered, casting long shadows across tired faces. Elias sat near the embers, muscles aching, thoughts swirling.

Martha sat beside him, breaking the quiet. "You carry too much alone."

He shook his head, managing a tired smile. "Not alone. Never alone."

The stars began to pierce the darkness, each one a distant beacon of hope. Elias looked up, finding strength in their cold light.

Tomorrow would bring new battles, new losses. But for now, they had held the line. And sometimes, that was enough.

The embers of battle still clung to the air. Smoke drifted in low curls across the forest floor, and the sharp scent of black powder mixed with pine sap and the iron tang of blood. Though the skirmish had ended, the echo of gunfire haunted the trees.

Elias sat alone on the edge of camp, his musket across his lap and his back against a tree. His hands were still blackened with soot and dirt, his sleeves stiff with dried sweat. He'd wiped the worst of the blood from his face, but there was no cleaning the grimness from his expression. A knot of muscle pulsed at his jaw, and his leg bounced unconsciously.

Martha approached without a sound, slipping down beside him in the tall grass. She carried a tin cup of water, which she wordlessly offered. Elias took it and drank deeply.

"They're patching up the wounded," she said, glancing back toward camp. "Captain says we lost five. Two more might not make it through the night."

Elias closed his eyes. "We didn't expect them to move so fast. I should've—"

"No," she cut in, her voice firm. "You made the right call. If we hadn't been on that ridge when we were, it would've been worse. A lot worse."

He didn't answer right away. The wind stirred the leaves above, and somewhere a whip-poor-will called from deep within the woods. Finally, Elias spoke, his voice low. "One of them couldn't have been older than me. Maybe younger. When I looked down at him, I saw his face—mud and blood and fear. I didn't even think. I just pulled the trigger."

"That's war," Martha said, though her tone softened. "Doesn't matter how many times it happens—it never feels right. If it ever does... that's when you need to be afraid."

Elias stared into the trees. "I keep thinking about what Samuel would've done."

She paused. "What *would* he have done?"

"He'd have fought, same as I did. But afterward, he'd have said something that made us laugh, or shake our heads. He was good at that. He made things feel lighter." Elias sighed. "I'm not like that."

Martha reached down and tossed a pinecone into the fire. "No. You're different. You don't lead with your mouth—you lead with your spine. Quiet, steady, the kind of man others lean on when things start falling apart."

He turned to her, his voice uncertain. "You think they see me that way?"

"I do," she said. "And they do too. Ask Joseph. Ask any of them."

Footsteps crunched softly through the underbrush. Joseph appeared, his coat patched and damp, and a fresh bandage wrapped around his forearm. He gave them a crooked smile. "Thought I might find you two here. Captain Hawkins wants to talk tactics in the morning. Says the scouts saw movement near the river bend—could be more Redcoat regulars or Loyalist militia."

Elias stood slowly, working the stiffness from his knees. "He wants us to hold?"

"For now. Reinforcements are on the way, but it could be another two days. Maybe three."

"Then we hold," Elias said, voice steady now.

Joseph studied him for a moment. "You alright?"

Elias nodded. "I will be."

Joseph clapped him on the shoulder and turned to Martha. "You'll be with us at the river?"

"I'll be there before sunrise."

Joseph left them with a nod, his silhouette disappearing into the shadows. Elias and Martha lingered.

The stars above burned bright and sharp, undimmed by town lanterns or city smoke. The wilderness wrapped around them, ancient and indifferent.

Elias broke the silence. "I never told you what happened the night I left home."

Martha raised an eyebrow. "What happened?"

"I heard my father crying. He thought we were all asleep. But I could hear him downstairs, crying like a man who'd lost everything. I think—" Elias swallowed. "I think he'd finally accepted Samuel wasn't coming home. And then I left him too. Walked out the door while the fire still burned in the hearth."

Martha placed her hand gently over his. "You left to honor Samuel. Your father might have cried again, sure—but he'd be proud, Elias. Of you. Of the fight in you."

He looked at her, eyes searching hers. "Do you believe that?"

"I do."

They sat in silence after that, the fire between them crackling low.

The next morning broke cold and gray. Mist hugged the ground, curling around boots and rifle barrels. The forest was hushed again, but the air held the weight of something coming—something more than another skirmish.

Elias stood at the head of the company, eyes scanning the treeline. Their ranks were thinner than before, but those who remained stood straighter now, united by survival, hardened by fire.

Captain Hawkins strode up beside him. "Our scouts report enemy movement north of the ridge. They may try to encircle us from the river pass."

Elias nodded. "We've got good cover there—fallen trees, brush, and a narrow crossing. If we can bottleneck them, we might stand a chance."

"I'm putting you in charge of the forward line," Hawkins said, voice crisp. "Joseph takes the rear guard. Martha will manage the sharpshooters. They'll set up in the trees. We hit fast, hit hard, then fall back and regroup."

Elias felt his chest tighten. "Understood."

As the company assembled, Martha approached, adjusting the strap on her powder horn. "You ready?"

He gave a grim smile. "No. But we go anyway."

She squeezed his arm, and then was gone, vanishing into the brush with her sharpshooters.

Elias turned to his line. Boys and men, farmers and smiths, woodsmen and widowers—they all waited for his word. Some clutched muskets like lifelines; others wore blades strapped across their chests.

"We hold the pass," Elias said. "Not because we're ordered to. Not because of glory or pay. We hold it for each other. For the men we lost. For the families behind us."

A murmur of agreement rose from the ranks.

Elias took his place at the front, just behind the fallen logs that would serve as their barricade. The trees whispered above them. The air grew still.

And then, from the far woods, came the sound of marching.

Ash crept over the horizon like breath on glass, veiling the world in a hush that seemed not to break, even with the stirring of men. Elias sat propped against a damp log, legs outstretched, his boots untied. He'd barely slept— only closed his eyes long enough to dream of nothing, which somehow left him even more tired than before. Around him, the Overmountain camp roused in slow motion. No calls, no drums. Just whispers. The kind of quiet that comes before something enormous.

Colonel Shelby passed by first, silent and expressionless, adjusting the clasp on his weathered coat. Beside him, Colonel Campbell wore his usual scowl of concentration, brow drawn so tightly that Elias wondered if he'd ever seen the man smile. Behind them, a line of scouts, mud-slicked and lean-eyed, gave nods to each other as they checked weapons and cinched gear. There was a language in their glances, and Elias, new to all this, could only guess at its meaning. He pulled his blanket tighter, watching, trying to make sense of the rhythm.

"They'll hit at first light," Jesse murmured beside him. The older boy crouched near the embers of their shared fire, blade in hand, sharpening it with slow, even strokes.

"Why wait?" Elias asked, voice hoarse from sleep and nerves.

"To see," Jesse replied. "To know where they stand. You can't charge blind into a fog and expect to come out the other side." He glanced up, giving Elias a small smile. "Though that's pretty much what we've been doing the whole way here, ain't it?"

Elias didn't return the smile. His gut felt like it was twisting in on itself, the dread creeping back up his spine. His hands had stopped shaking during the march, but now that they weren't moving, the tremble returned. He rubbed them together for warmth—and steadiness.

Further up the ridge, Colonel Sevier had gathered a knot of men around him. He was speaking in low tones, gesturing toward the slope beyond which Ferguson's Loyalists waited. The mention of the British major's name made Elias straighten. Ferguson was just a shadow to him still, but one that loomed large. He'd heard stories—of brutality and pride, of warnings sent like thunderclaps across the mountains. "Lay down your arms or be destroyed," the man had said. The Overmountain Men had chosen the latter.

The scouts returned with news before the sun had fully broken through the trees.

"He's still camped below," one of them reported. "Guard's posted, but not expecting a storm."

Campbell gave a nod. "Then we bring one."

Orders flowed swiftly after that. Men assembled without shouting. Boots snapped into place. Packs were lightened and left behind. Elias found himself gripping his musket tighter than ever before, not because it gave him comfort, but because letting go of it now felt like admitting fear.

In the ranks, silence returned like a breath held in unison. Jesse stood to his left. Behind them, the younger boys from Watauga, the ones who had once looked at Elias like he was just a blacksmith's son, now wore the same eyes he did—uncertain, wide, waiting.

A single bird called out from the forest. Then came the order: "Forward."

They moved like a flood. A controlled, ruthless swell of men pushing down the slope. Wet leaves crackled beneath their boots, the sound faint against the pounding in Elias's ears. The smell of cold earth and old smoke filled his lungs. And there—through the break in the trees—the first glimpse of the enemy camp. Tents, fire pits, horses stamping in confusion. Ferguson's redcoats were there, scattered among Loyalist militia. Unaware.

Until the Overmountain Men opened fire.

The ridge exploded with gunfire, every musket a voice raised in defiance. Elias aimed without thinking. He saw a man in a blue coat stand—then fall. The recoil hit him like a kick, but he reloaded by instinct, powder and ball moving from pouch to barrel in one swift, shaky motion. The air stank of sulfur. Men shouted. Orders blurred.

Ferguson's men responded quickly, returning fire from behind wagons and hastily overturned barrels. One of the Overmountain Men near Elias staggered back, clutching his leg with a grimace. Jesse grabbed him by the collar and dragged him behind a fallen tree. Elias watched, frozen, until someone shouted at him to move up.

He did.

The ground flattened ahead, then dropped into a hollow. Elias and a dozen others pressed forward, firing, ducking, loading, again and again. He couldn't tell who was winning. All he saw were faces—some young, some grizzled, all fighting like the ground beneath them was home itself.

And then he saw the banner.

Ferguson's command flag flapped near the center of the Loyalist camp. A cluster of men guarded it, crouched behind stacked barrels. There, atop a white horse, sat the British major. Dressed in bright red and brass, he was unmistakable. His voice boomed over the din, barking orders in a clipped, furious accent.

"There!" someone yelled. "Ferguson!"

Shots rang out. The major's horse reared. Ferguson turned—his pistol raised—and fired into the trees. Elias saw him fall a moment later, his body tumbling into the mud like a sack of corn.

A shout went up. It wasn't clear if it was Overmountain men or Ferguson's Loyalists who cried out first, but the sound was the same: finality.

The center crumbled.

The Loyalists broke. Some surrendered. Others fled. A few kept fighting, but the edge was gone. Colonel Campbell charged forward, waving his hat. "Take the camp!" he roared.

Elias moved as if in a trance. His musket was empty. He didn't remember firing the last shot. All around him, men surged forward, claiming the enemy ground like a tidal wave swallowing the beach. The smell of powder hung thick, but behind it, Elias could sense something else—relief. Or maybe disbelief.

It was over.

He dropped to his knees beside a tree stump, breath ragged, arms trembling.

His face was streaked with soot and sweat. He didn't know how long he sat there before Jesse found him.

"You good?" the older boy asked.

Elias nodded.

"You hit?"

"No."

Jesse sat down beside him, pulling a flask from his coat. "We did it."

Elias looked around. The ridge was littered with broken gear, torn flags, and the unmoving bodies of both friend and foe. Victory didn't look like he'd imagined. It wasn't cheers or celebration. It was silence. A kind of numb awe. The price lay all around them.

He closed his eyes and let the cold air wash over him. Not far off, he heard someone begin to sing—a low, tired tune, like something remembered from childhood.

Elias didn't join in. He just listened, letting the sound carry him through the morning, through the memory, through the weight of what they had done.

Smoke lingered over the ridge long after the guns had fallen silent. It drifted between the trees like a ghost unsure where to rest, a pale veil clinging to the leaves and branches, casting everything in a strange, silver-gray light. Morning had fully broken, but the sun had no warmth left to offer.

Elias stood near the center of what had once been the Loyalist camp. Now, it was a shattered collection of torn tents, smoldering wagons, and the bodies of men. A few moaned where they lay wounded—some begging for water, others whispering the names of wives and mothers they would never see again.

He had not imagined victory would feel like this.

Colonel Campbell moved among the wounded, issuing soft orders. Sevier and Shelby were with him, speaking in low tones, their expressions tight. None of them smiled. There was no celebration, only the grim duty of aftermath.

"We bury them all," Sevier said, his voice clipped. "Ours and theirs. Let no man lie unmarked on this mountain."

Jesse was nearby, shirt sleeves rolled, helping move the dead. His face was streaked with soot and something darker. Blood, maybe. Not his. His hands trembled, but he kept working.

Elias approached him quietly.

"You alright?" he asked.

Jesse didn't answer at first. He stared at the body in front of him—a boy no older than Elias, a musket still clutched in stiff fingers, his eyes open to the sky.

"We were both fifteen," Jesse finally said. "I asked him. Just before the first volley. He was from Ninety Six."

Elias swallowed hard. "Did he say his name?"

"No." Jesse looked up. "He died quick. Some don't."

They lifted the boy together, carried him to the edge of the clearing where the others were being laid in rows. There were no markers yet, just lines of men in silence, the forest bearing witness.

Behind them, a group of Overmountain Men worked to dig graves. It was slow going—the earth rocky, the tools dull. But no one complained. They worked like penance.

Others stood off to the side, staring. One man—Elias recognized him as from Watauga—was weeping openly, holding a scrap of cloth in his hands. Another had sunk to his knees, fingers tangled in his beard, praying in a language Elias didn't know.

It felt like the world had been hollowed out.

Elias walked through the camp alone for a while, avoiding the worst of the carnage. The ground was churned up, blood darkening the soil. He spotted a broken drum, a trampled Bible, a hat hanging from a low branch like someone had set it there carefully and forgotten it in the chaos.

A movement caught his eye—a Loyalist officer, wounded but alive, propped against a wagon wheel. His uniform was soaked with blood, and his face pale as paper. He held a hand out as Elias passed.

"Water," the man croaked.

Elias hesitated, then knelt and offered his canteen. The officer drank greedily, gasping between gulps.

"Name?" Elias asked, though he didn't know why.

"Thomas Green," the man rasped. "Georgia. Thought we'd have the hill... thought we'd..." He coughed, blood flecking his lips.

Elias said nothing. What was there to say?

"Tell... tell them I fought like a soldier," Green whispered, as if needing that to be known. "Not a traitor. Just... a different flag."

Elias nodded, though his throat was tight.

He stayed until the man stopped breathing.

By midday, the burial had begun. The Overmountain Men lined up, each grave filled with not just bodies, but memories too heavy to speak. Some men whispered prayers. Others wept openly. Elias helped where he could—hauling dirt, folding arms across chests, removing belts and knives so they wouldn't be buried with blades.

No one spoke of glory.

It was late afternoon before the last body was laid to rest. The grave markers were crude—stones, sticks, sometimes just a ring of branches. But they were something. Proof that these men, no matter their side, had existed.

Colonel Shelby called the remaining men together near the ridge's edge.

"We have done what we came to do," he said. "Ferguson is dead. His threat against our mountains is ended."

A murmur went through the ranks. No cheers.

"We've lost good men," Shelby continued. "Boys. Fathers. Brothers. And though we've struck a great blow, let no one walk away from this hill unchanged."

Colonel Campbell stepped forward next. "Take this day into your bones," he said, voice firm. "And remember—war leaves no man as it found him."

Then they dismissed the ranks.

Elias didn't move right away. He stood watching the trees sway in the afternoon light, the wind carrying ash and pine together in an almost sweet scent. He didn't feel like a boy anymore. But he didn't feel like a man either. Something else. Something in between.

Jesse joined him.

"We should head down soon," he said. "Before dark."

Elias nodded. "Yeah."

They walked the edge of the ridge in silence for a while, looking down at the valley below. Somewhere out there, news of Ferguson's fall would spread like fire through the hills. The British would feel it. The Loyalists would scatter. And the Overmountain Men would return to farms, forges, and cabins, forever altered.

"I don't want to forget him," Elias said suddenly.

"Who?"

"That boy. The one from Ninety Six."

Jesse nodded. "Then don't."

They turned back toward the camp. Fires were burning again—small, warming, meant for food not war. The smell of coffee mixed with woodsmoke. It felt like a different world than the one they'd woken to that morning.

Before they reached their gear, Elias paused. He pulled the worn letter from his coat—the one from Samuel, faded and creased from so many readings.

He read it again now, the words harder than ever to hold:

Elias, if I don't come back, promise me you'll be strong. Not just with your hands, but your heart too. There's more to winning than fighting. There's what comes after. The world you shape with what's left.

He folded it carefully and put it away.

The mountain had taken something from him. But it had given something too—clarity, maybe. Or purpose. He didn't yet know.

But he would.

Chapter 12

A heavy stillness hung over the rugged hills, the smoke of past fires curling through the trees. Elias stirred beneath a wool blanket, damp with dew and stained from yesterday's blood. The wind, soft as breath, brushed against his cheek, carrying with it the acrid scent of black powder and the earthier tang of churned-up mud. His eyes opened slowly, reluctant to face what daylight might reveal.

Around him, the field lay quiet—not in peace, but in exhaustion. The cannon thunder was gone, as were the shouts, the cries, the deafening crack of muskets. In their place was something worse: the low groans of the wounded, the shuffle of boots moving through grass, and the occasional sob, muffled by distance or dignity.

Elias sat up, his back stiff and muscles sore. The world tilted as he rose, the adrenaline that had carried him through the chaos now gone, leaving only trembling limbs and a churning stomach. He scanned the horizon. King's Mountain, that cruel ridge of rock and trees, loomed behind him, still casting its long shadow over the bloody slope.

He remembered little after the final charge. Just flashes: the recoil of his musket, the moment Isaac fell, a Loyalist's eyes wide in surprise as Elias pulled the trigger. He had lost his hat somewhere in the scramble, and his coat was torn across the left sleeve. A shallow cut ran from elbow to wrist, mostly dried now, more of a memory than a wound.

"Elias?" a voice called from behind. He turned to see Thomlin, his friend from the river march, limping toward him. His left arm was bound in a crude sling made from a woman's shawl, and he had dried blood on his temple.

"You alive?" Thomlin asked, voice hoarse but laced with relief.

"I think so," Elias said. "Are you?"

"Barely. Doc Renfrow says I was lucky. Bullet grazed me. Isaac's with the others. He made it."

Elias exhaled. "Thank God."

They walked together toward the ridge, where bodies still lay in twisted heaps—some in blue, some in brown and gray. The Loyalists had been pinned against the top, nowhere to run, many shot where they stood. Some of the Overmountain Men still prowled the slope, poking through pockets, retrieving powder, or making grim notes of the dead. Others knelt in prayer or silence.

Elias stopped beside one man—barely older than he was—sprawled face-down on the roots of an oak tree. The man's tricorne hat had fallen beside him, and blood pooled beneath his chest. A makeshift haversack was slung across his back, the flap torn open to reveal a tattered Bible and a bundle of letters tied with twine.

He crouched beside the body and hesitated before closing the man's eyes. He couldn't say why—it just felt like the right thing to do. As his hand brushed the cold skin, a shiver ran down his spine.

Thomlin stood a few feet away, watching. "Don't look too long," he said softly. "Or it'll follow you home."

Elias stood, fists clenched. "He was someone. They all were."

Thomlin nodded, but his gaze drifted away. "Aye. But the war don't care."

They walked farther, passing makeshift bandage stations and groups of men dragging branches to start fires. Someone had lined up bodies along a ridge line—Loyalist and Patriot alike—and was covering them with tarps. The sun, pale and cold, began to rise higher, revealing more detail than Elias cared to see.

He stopped when he saw a familiar shape near a burnt stump. It was Josiah, kneeling beside a still body, his rifle laid across his lap like a sleeping child. His head was bowed, and his shoulders trembled. Elias approached slowly, recognizing the fallen man as one of the Carolina volunteers. He didn't ask the name.

Josiah looked up when Elias reached him. His face was lined with tears and dirt.

"He saved my life," Josiah whispered. "Twice. And now—"

Elias knelt beside him and laid a hand on his shoulder. "I'm sorry."

The silence that followed wasn't awkward or empty—it was sacred. They stayed there until the burial bell rang from the ridge, signaling the start of the first service.

"Come on," Elias said gently. "We'll stand for him."

Josiah nodded and rose, wiping his face with the back of his hand. Together, they made their way toward the sound of prayer.

No flags were raised in triumph. No drums beat a song of glory. Victory had come not with cheers, but with silence—and with the grim work of reckoning.

The wounded lay in rows across the clearing, wrapped in spare linens, hides, or nothing at all. Cries of pain broke through the still morning as the makeshift surgeons moved from man to man, knives and saws clutched in trembling hands. There were no antiseptics. No anesthesia. Just a bottle of whiskey, a steady arm, and whatever prayers a man could remember.

Elias found himself carrying water from a nearby spring, cupping it with his hands when no vessel could be spared. He knelt by a soldier from Georgia whose leg was gone from the knee down, wrapped in blood-soaked cloth. The man didn't speak, didn't even look at Elias—just stared into some place beyond the trees, his jaw clenched tight. Elias offered water. The man took it, but only drank a sip.

Not far away, Isaac and two other boys—barely older than Elias—dug graves with short-handled spades. The ground was hard, thick with roots, and they worked in near silence. No one spoke unless necessary. There were too many names to remember, too many faces already fading from memory. So they buried them in rows, sometimes with markers, sometimes with none.

Thomlin approached Elias with two loaves of corn bread and a side of smoked rabbit, wrapped in oilcloth. "They're calling it a feast," he said, with a grim smile.

Elias sat with him beneath a red maple, its leaves already turning. He ate slowly, chewing more from the need to move his jaw than from hunger. His mouth was dry. The food stuck to his throat.

"Did you see Major Ferguson's body?" Thomlin asked quietly.

Elias shook his head.

"Shot through the chest. Some say seven, eight times. They found him tangled under his horse, dead before he hit the ground. His men tried to surrender, but we gave no quarter." He paused. "Can't say I blame anyone. After what they did in the Carolinas..."

Elias remembered the stories: the burned farms, the hangings without trial, the Loyalist raids through frontier towns. Some said Ferguson had promised to lay the region to waste. Others said he merely enforced the Crown's will. Either way, he'd met his end on that hillside.

"He's being buried today," Thomlin continued. "Up on the ridge. Some of the men wanted to hang his body, leave it for the birds. But Colonel Shelby ordered it done proper."

Elias nodded. "War doesn't make men better."

"No. It just shows us what we already are."

They finished the meal in silence. Around them, men sharpened knives, repacked ammunition, or simply sat and stared into the trees. The atmosphere was heavy—not just with grief, but with something deeper, something close to guilt. Not everyone had fought for glory. Many had come to protect their homes, their kin, to stand against tyranny. But in the slaughter of victory, it was hard to tell the righteous from the savage.

Later that afternoon, Colonel Campbell gathered the men at the edge of the battlefield. He stood tall, but his face was pale and sun-worn, as though he'd aged five years in a day. He waited until the murmurs died down before speaking.

"Brothers," he said, voice carrying across the slope. "We came here to end a threat. And we have done so. Ferguson is dead. His force is broken. The Crown's grip on our land has loosened, and word of this day will carry far and wide."

A few men nodded. Others looked away.

"But let none of us mistake this for the end. This war is far from done. There will be more fighting. More dying. We must return home, regroup, and prepare for what comes next."

He paused, letting the weight of his words settle.

"Honor the dead. Care for the wounded. And may God have mercy on all of us."

That evening, Elias stood alone at the crest of King's Mountain, looking down at the slope where it had all ended. The golden light of sunset bathed the trees, turning the leaves to fire. The ridge was quiet now, save for the soft songs rising from the burial teams. One of them—a hymn he knew from childhood—reached his ears:

Come, ye weary, heavy laden...

Elias whispered the words along with them, his voice catching in his throat.

Footsteps crunched behind him. He turned to see Josiah, his hat in his hands, eyes red-rimmed but dry.

"They're burning the Loyalist supplies," Josiah said. "Ammunition, wagons, even their food."

"Waste," Elias muttered.

"Shelby says it's to keep it from falling into other Loyalist hands."

Elias sighed and looked back over the ridge. "Doesn't feel like winning."

Josiah shrugged. "Maybe that's what winning is."

They stood in silence until the stars began to appear, faint and flickering in the growing dusk. Then Josiah broke it with a question Elias had asked himself more than once.

"What'll you do when this is over?"

Elias thought of the forge, the anvil, the familiar heat of home. He thought of his mother's hands, rough from labor, and of Samuel's grave beneath the apple tree. He thought of what he'd carry back with him—what weight he'd never shake off.

"I'll go home," he said. "If home's still there."

Josiah nodded, looking toward the east. "Ain't nothing going to be the same."

"No," Elias agreed. "But we can try."

And in that moment, with the wind cold against their backs and the stars growing brighter overhead, Elias felt the truth of it settle deep in his bones. This wasn't the end of anything. It was just the beginning of another kind of fight.

Rain fell in the night. Not a storm, not the kind that comes with thunder and shouting skies, but a soft, steady weep—like the earth was mourning what had been spilled upon it.

By morning, the battlefield had turned to mud. Blood had pooled in the low places and mixed with ash from the burned wagons, forming a paste that clung to boots and wouldn't wash off. Elias scraped it from his soles with a stick as he watched the last of the prisoners being marched out under guard. Around thirty remained from the nearly two hundred taken. The rest—those deemed guilty of atrocities or identified as part of Ferguson's raiding parties—had already been executed. No trial. Just a command, a rope, and a tree.

Some men cheered when the hangings happened. Others turned away. Elias did neither. He simply watched, jaw tight, hands clenched at his sides. He told himself that justice had been done, that those men had brought it upon themselves—but still, he couldn't forget their eyes. Some were young. Too young. Boys who'd chosen the wrong side because someone told them it was the right one.

Now they dangled from poplars like forgotten fruit.

Shelby's men moved quickly to break camp. Word had come that Cornwallis was repositioning near the Catawba, and the Overmountain Men had no desire to be caught unprepared. By noon, Elias had packed his bedroll and lashed it to his back with fresh leather thongs. He'd mended his boots with strips of hide and patched a hole in his shirt with a square of linen taken from a discarded tent flap.

As he worked, Colonel Sevier passed by. The man looked more gaunt than ever, his beard streaked with ash and his coat still splattered with dried blood.

Yet his eyes—sharp, blue, watchful—remained alert. He paused when he saw Elias.

"You carried yourself well, son."

Elias stood straight. "Thank you, Colonel."

"You ride back with the Carolina line or with Campbell?"

"I'll ride with whoever's heading west."

Sevier nodded, then reached into his satchel and pulled out a folded piece of paper. "This came from Captain McDowell. He asked it be passed to a boy named Elias McCrae."

Elias took the letter with both hands, heart catching. "Thank you."

Sevier didn't linger. He moved on down the line, shouting orders and directing wagons toward the riverbank.

Elias sat beneath a pine tree and unfolded the letter. The paper was creased and smudged, the handwriting stiff but legible.

Elias,

If you're reading this, it means you've made it through. I knew you would. You've the heart for this life, even if I wish you didn't.

I'll be returning home soon. My brother was killed near Camden, and I've a farm to manage now. I imagine the same might be true for you.

There's no glory in what we've done. Only consequence. But know this: you stood among men, and you didn't break. That matters.

If ever you come east again, stop by. The door will be open.

– Captain McDowell

Elias folded the letter slowly and tucked it into the inside of his shirt, next to his skin.

"Everything all right?" came a voice.

It was Isaac, his arms full of firewood, eyes curious.

Elias nodded. "Yeah. Just... a reminder."

They built a small fire that night, despite orders to keep the light low. The rain had passed, but the cold had not, and the men needed warmth. Around the flickering flame, they gathered—Thomlin, Josiah, Isaac, and a few others who'd survived the mountain. Some had wounds; some bore only the invisible kind. Yet all shared the same silence, the kind that comes after the unthinkable has happened and you're still breathing.

"Anybody know what day it is?" Josiah asked, poking the fire with a stick.

"October," someone mumbled. "Fifteenth, maybe?"

"Feels longer," Isaac said. "Feels like a whole year's passed since we crossed the gap."

Thomlin chuckled. "I still remember Elias stumbling into the fire the first night."

Elias rolled his eyes. "I remember your snoring kept half the ridge awake."

That brought a laugh from a few, small but real. The fire crackled. Sparks rose into the night, carried upward by wind and memory.

Josiah reached into his coat and pulled out a flask. "To Samuel," he said, voice low.

Elias froze.

Josiah looked across the flames. "You mentioned him once, that first week. Said he was your brother. Said you were walking for both of you."

Elias nodded slowly, throat tight. "He died at Musgrove Mill. Shot in the river. Never came home."

They passed the flask in silence, each man taking a small swig. When it came back to Elias, he hesitated.

Then he raised it slightly, voice no more than a whisper. "To Samuel. And to all who won't be riding home."

He drank.

Afterward, they lay in their blankets, backs to the wind, eyes on the stars.

"I don't know what waits for us back home," Isaac said, quietly. "But I don't think we'll ever be the same."

Elias didn't answer. He didn't have to. They all felt it—that the war had taken something from them, something they hadn't even known was vulnerable.

But in its place, something else had formed. A bond not of friendship, or even brotherhood, but of understanding. The kind that comes only to those who've seen the same fire and survived it.

As the fire died down to embers, Elias turned onto his side, staring at the hills they'd soon leave behind. He thought of home, of the forge, of the iron tools his father had shaped and the bellows Samuel used to pump air through the coals.

And then he thought of the vow he'd made on the trail—that if he lived through this, he'd not let it be for nothing.

He would go home. He would remember. And he would forge something better.

Something worthy of the sacrifice.

The morning air was sharp with frost as Elias rolled his bedroll and prepared to move out. The firelight had long since faded, leaving only the pale glow of dawn filtering through the skeletal branches of the pines. The ground beneath his feet was frozen in patches, stiff and hard after the recent rain and cold night.

Men bustled around the camp, the clang of steel on wood, the creak of wagon wheels, and the low murmur of conversation filling the crisp air. The army was stirring, preparing to break from the battlefield for the last time. The march back home would be long—longer than the way in, filled with weariness and quiet reckoning.

Elias adjusted the straps of his pack and glanced toward the river's edge where wagons were lining up. The Catawba lay still and gray, its surface like glass broken only by the occasional flick of a fish or the ripple of a duck taking flight. Somewhere beyond that river, back east, the war churned on. But here, on this land scarred by fire and blood, the war felt closer to its end.

Colonel Sevier stood near the camp command, barking last-minute orders and making sure the wounded were loaded onto wagons and stretched across carts. Despite the lines of exhaustion drawn on his face, there was an unmistakable steel beneath his eyes—a resolve that had seen them through the darkest days.

Elias hesitated for a moment before stepping forward. "Colonel," he said, voice steady but low.

Sevier turned and looked down at him, eyes narrowing with a mix of tiredness and recognition. "McCrae. You ready?"

"I am. But I wanted to ask—what now? After this?"

The older man's lips tightened. "We've fought a hard fight, Elias. We've broken the back of Ferguson's raid and sent a message to Cornwallis. But the war isn't over—not by far. We go home now, but we keep watch. We rebuild. And we remember."

Elias nodded. "I understand."

Sevier's gaze softened briefly. "Good. You've got more grit than most. You'll be needed."

The march began soon after, the steady rumble of wagon wheels and horses breaking the silence. Elias fell into step beside Isaac and Josiah, their faces set in lines of exhaustion but also relief. The Overmountain Men had survived the battle and the brutal aftermath. They had endured.

As they crossed the river on a makeshift ferry, Elias looked back once at the battlefield — now a quiet expanse of mud and fallen trees, the smoke long gone but the memory still fresh. A knot tightened in his stomach, and he pulled his coat tighter around himself.

"This won't be the last time we see this land," Isaac said quietly, reading Elias's thoughts.

"No," Elias replied. "But I hope it's the last time we see it soaked in blood."

The days that followed were grueling. The trail home was rugged and worn, marked by stony ridges, tangled forests, and swollen streams. The army moved slowly, ever watchful for enemy patrols or guerrilla fighters. Cold seeped into their bones, and the food ran low, forcing the men to ration and scavenge what they could.

Along the way, Elias found himself thinking less about the fighting and more about what awaited at home. Would his family still be there? Would the forge still burn? And what of Samuel's memory—how would it be honored in the quiet days to come?

One evening, as the sun dipped below the horizon, Elias sat beside the campfire with Josiah and Isaac. The firelight flickered across their tired faces.

"Think you'll go back to smithing when this is done?" Josiah asked, breaking the silence.

Elias smiled faintly. "I have to. It's all I know."

Isaac shook his head. "You've changed, Elias. You're not the boy who left the mountain months ago."

"Neither are you," Elias said, meeting his friend's gaze.

"We all carry something now," Isaac said. "Wounds we can't see."

The three sat quietly, the crackling fire a small comfort against the vast wilderness around them.

When they finally reached the foothills of the Appalachians, the men paused to rest. The familiar smell of pine and damp earth was a balm to Elias's frayed nerves. Each step brought memories flooding back—of laughter shared, of promises made and broken, of brothers lost.

A courier arrived one afternoon with news that Cornwallis had withdrawn further south, his forces weakened but not defeated. The war would drag on, but here, in these rugged mountains, the Overmountain Men had carved their place in history.

Elias stood atop a ridge overlooking the valley, the land stretching out like a patchwork quilt of farms, rivers, and small settlements. Somewhere down there was his home, the forge, and the family that awaited him.

He clenched his fists, determination filling him anew.

No matter what came next, he would carry the fire of this fight inside him. The forge of war had tempered him, and though the steel was hot, it would be shaped by his hands.

A new chapter awaited—one not of battle, but of rebuilding and hope.

As night fell, Elias settled beneath a starry sky, the sounds of the forest soothing his restless mind. He breathed deeply, the cold air filling his lungs.

Tomorrow, the long road home would continue. But tonight, he was alive. And that was enough.

Morning light crept slowly over the rolling hills as the Overmountain Men packed up camp for the final leg of their journey. The air was cool but tinged with a quiet optimism. Even the birds seemed to chirp a little brighter, as if sensing the end of their long march. Elias tightened the straps on his pack, feeling the weight not only of his gear but of the months behind him—the battles, the losses, and the hard-earned victories.

The road home was no easy path. Mud churned underfoot where rain had soaked the earth. Fallen trees and jagged rocks forced the wagon wheels to creak and groan. But the men pressed on with steady determination, their minds filled with visions of hearth and home, faces of loved ones waiting at the journey's end.

Beside Elias, Josiah rode his horse with a quiet steadiness. "You think we'll recognize everything when we get back?" Josiah asked, glancing over with a tired smile.

Elias shrugged. "Maybe not everything. But the land, the mountains—they'll still be here. Same as before. It's the people that change."

Isaac, walking just behind them, nodded. "And we've changed too. This war has marked us all. Some scars run deeper than others."

As the men moved, they shared stories from the road—tales of skirmishes, close calls, and moments of unexpected kindness. The laughter was scarce but genuine, a balm for worn souls.

Elias's thoughts often drifted to his family—his mother's steady hands, his father's quiet pride, and the empty place Samuel's absence had left. He wondered how the forge was faring, whether the flames still danced as bright as before.

The day grew warmer, and the sun climbed higher, casting long shadows across the forest floor. When the column reached the outskirts of a small settlement, the familiar sight of a church steeple rising above the treetops made Elias's heart leap.

"Home," he whispered.

A slow smile spread across Josiah's face. "Almost there."

As they approached the village, children spilled out from cottages and fields, their eyes wide with wonder at the ragged soldiers passing through. Women stood at doorways, clutching shawls and wiping tears. The weight of the moment settled heavy over Elias.

When they finally reached the edge of the village, Elias spotted a figure waiting near the smithy—his mother, her hands folded tightly, eyes scanning the road for any sign of her son. At the sight of Elias, her face broke into a radiant smile. Without hesitation, she rushed forward, enveloping him in an embrace that brought tears to both their eyes.

"Elias," she whispered, her voice trembling. "You're home."

The forge, though worn by time and the absence of its master, still stood solid—its stone hearth dark but ready. Elias ran his hand over the familiar tools, each one telling stories of sweat and fire, of shaping metal and shaping a life.

Over the following days, Elias helped tend to the smithy, rebuilding what had fallen into disrepair. Each strike of the hammer echoed like a heartbeat, steady and strong. The rhythm was soothing, a reminder that life could be rebuilt, even after war.

Neighbors visited, offering congratulations and sharing news of the battles that had shaped their world. Elias listened, absorbing the stories and weaving them into his own.

One evening, as the sun dipped behind the mountains, Elias sat beside the hearth with Josiah and Isaac. The fire crackled warmly, casting dancing shadows on their faces.

"War changes a man," Isaac said softly. "But it doesn't have to define him."

Elias nodded. "It's what we do after the fighting that matters most."

Josiah raised his cup. "To the future—whatever it may hold."

They drank, the warmth of friendship and hope filling the room.

In the days that followed, Elias found himself visiting Samuel's grave. The simple wooden cross stood among wildflowers, a quiet testament to a brother lost but never forgotten.

"I'll carry you with me," Elias said, kneeling by the grave. "In every hammer strike, every breath."

The valley around him was alive with the sounds of spring—birds singing, leaves rustling in the breeze, and the distant murmur of the river. Life, fragile and fierce, pushed forward.

Elias looked toward the horizon, the mountains standing tall and eternal.

His journey had changed him, forged him like steel in the fire. But home was where the heart lay, and here he would rebuild—not just a life, but a legacy.

The war was over, but the story was just beginning.

Epilogue

The sun rose gently over the valley, spilling golden light across fields waking from a long, cold winter. Birds sang their morning songs, weaving melodies through the crisp air as the village stirred to life. Elias stood at the forge, the familiar warmth of the fire flickering against his face. Years had passed since the march and the battles, but the rhythm of hammer against anvil still echoed deep in his bones.

Around him, the village bustled with quiet determination. Homes repaired, fields plowed, and children's laughter ringing through the streets—life after war was not easy, but it was theirs to reclaim.

Elias wiped sweat from his brow, setting aside his hammer to watch a group of young boys gathered nearby. They listened intently as he showed them how to shape a horseshoe, his hands steady and sure.

"Remember," Elias said, voice low but firm, "metal bends and twists, but with patience and care, it becomes strong. The same goes for us."

One boy, no older than ten, looked up with wide eyes. "Will I be as strong as you someday, Mr. McCrae?"

Elias smiled. "Stronger. You've got fire in you."

The forge's heat was comforting, a reminder of the life he built from ashes and loss. Beside him, his old hammer sat—scarred but steady, like the man who wielded it. Every scar told a story: battles fought, friends lost, lessons learned.

Beyond the village, the mountains stood guard—silent witnesses to a land shaped by history and hope.

Elias turned to the open road, imagining the future unfolding like the horizon before him. Life would bring new challenges, but here, in the place he called home, he had found purpose.

A child's laughter broke through his thoughts, and Elias knelt to meet a small girl running toward him, her curls bouncing with each step.

"Papa!" she cried, throwing her arms around his waist.

His heart swelled with a joy that no battle could diminish.

"Hello, little one," he said, lifting her into his arms. "Ready to learn about fire and steel?"

Her bright eyes shone. "Yes, Papa. Teach me."

As the sun climbed higher, Elias knew the forge's flame would never die—not as long as the next generation carried its light.

Evening settled over the village like a soft blanket, cooling the earth and coaxing stars to peek through the darkening sky. Lanterns flickered outside humble homes, and a quiet hum of voices gathered near the clearing where a simple stone monument stood. The village had carved the names of the Overmountain Men who'd marched and fought, etched deep into granite—a testament to courage, sacrifice, and unyielding hope.

Elias approached the monument, his footsteps soft against the grass, the weight of years pressing on his chest. Beside him, neighbors and friends came to join—a community bound by shared grief and pride.

Children stood quietly, their faces solemn in the firelight. Old men and women whispered stories—some familiar, some new—of days when muskets cracked like thunder and hearts beat like war drums.

Elias's gaze fell on a name near the center: *Samuel McCrae.*

A tight knot formed in his throat. His brother's memory was a flame that neither time nor distance could dim.

He knelt and placed a hand on the cool stone, fingers tracing the carved letters.

"Samuel," Elias whispered, "you fought with honor. You showed me the way."

A woman stepped forward, carrying a small bundle wrapped in cloth. It was a flag, folded carefully, worn but whole.

"We honor them all," she said, voice steady despite the tears glistening in her eyes. "Their fight was for freedom, for the future."

Elias nodded; his thoughts drifting to the days of hardship—the march through rugged mountains, the camaraderie forged in fire and blood, the bitter moments of loss.

Around the fire, voices rose in song, a ballad passed down by those who remembered the battle. It told of bravery, of ordinary men turned heroes, of a dream kindled beneath a smoky sky.

Listening, Elias felt the weight of history settle gently on his shoulders—a mantle of responsibility and hope.

After the song faded, the village elder, a gray-haired man with eyes sharp as flint, stepped forward.

"We carry their story," he said. "Not just in stone, but in the lives we live, the choices we make."

Elias met his gaze. The future wasn't just about remembrance—it was about living the legacy.

As the crowd slowly dispersed, Elias lingered a moment longer. He looked up at the stars now fully shining above, and with a quiet breath, promised himself to keep their memory alive—not as ghosts of the past, but as guides lighting the path ahead.

Morning light filtered softly through the windows of Elias's modest home, painting the wooden floor with patterns of gold and shadow. The room smelled faintly of fresh bread and pine smoke, a peaceful contrast to the echoes of war that still lingered beyond these walls.

At the sturdy oak table, Elias sat with his young daughter, Sarah, her bright eyes fixed on an old, worn journal spread before them. The pages were filled with letters, sketches, and tales from the march—words that carried the weight of history and the spark of hope.

"Tell me again about Uncle Samuel," Sarah said, her voice curious and earnest.

Elias smiled, brushing a stray curl from her forehead. "Your uncle was brave—one of the first to step forward when the call came. He believed in fighting for a better tomorrow."

Sarah traced a finger along a faded drawing of mountains and men in line. "Did you miss him?"

A pause settled between them, filled with unspoken memories.

"Every day," Elias said softly. "But his spirit lives on in us—and in you."

The warmth between father and daughter was a living testament to survival and renewal. Outside, the village was stirring, children playing in the fields, neighbors greeting one another with smiles and hope.

Later, Elias walked through the village square, now vibrant with market stalls and laughter. The scars of war were slowly healing, replaced by the steady pulse of life and community.

He stopped by the forge, where a young apprentice was hard at work, shaping iron with careful hands.

"Remember, the fire teaches us patience," Elias said. "It burns steady when tended right."

The boy nodded, eyes shining with determination.

Turning toward the distant mountains, Elias felt a deep sense of peace. The land had borne witness to hardship and courage, to loss and renewal.

His heart swelled with pride—not just for the past, but for the future growing strong in the hands of the next generation.

As he gazed at the rising sun, Elias knew the story of the Overmountain Men was far from over. It lived on in every forged horseshoe, every shared story, every hopeful child's dream.

Seeds of tomorrow had been planted in the fertile soil of yesterday—and from them, a new dawn would rise.

Author's Note

Thank you for journeying with Elias and the Overmountain Men through a pivotal moment in American history. This story blends fact and fiction to bring to life the courage, sacrifice, and resilience of ordinary people who shaped the course of the Revolutionary War.

While Elias is a fictional character, his experiences are inspired by the real men and women who faced harsh wilderness, battle, and loss to defend their homes and ideals. My hope is that this novel offers a window into their struggles and triumphs, and invites reflection on the enduring values of freedom, community, and hope.

As you close this book, may you carry forward the legacy of those who marched before us—reminding us that history is not just in the past but lives in the choices we make today.

— Alex Gillespie

Historical Context

The Overmountain Men were frontier militia from the Appalachian regions of Virginia, North Carolina, and Tennessee who played a crucial role in the American Revolutionary War. In 1780, they organized a remarkable march over the rugged mountains to confront Loyalist forces at the Battle of Kings Mountain, a decisive Patriot victory.

This battle marked a turning point in the Southern campaign and is often remembered as a victory of citizen soldiers fighting for their land and liberty. The march itself was arduous, covering hundreds of miles through difficult terrain, with little formal training or supplies.

Many of the Overmountain Men were farmers, blacksmiths, and tradesmen—ordinary people who answered the call to defend their families and future. Their story exemplifies the spirit of grassroots resistance and the complexities of frontier life during the Revolution.

For more information and sources, readers are encouraged to explore historical records, letters, and personal accounts from the era, as well as visit sites like the Kings Mountain National Military Park.

www.ingramcontent.com/pod-product-compliance
Lightning Source LLC
Chambersburg PA
CBHW032309310726
48973CB00008B/2572